Seven Days to a Killing

Clive Egleton

CORONET BOOKS
Hodder Paperbacks Ltd., London

First published by
Hodder and Stoughton Ltd 1973
Coronet edition 1974
Second impression 1974

Printed in Great Britain
for Coronet Books, Hodder Paperbacks Ltd.,
St. Paul's House, Warwick Lane, London, EC4P 4AH,
by Richard Clay (The Chaucer Press), Ltd.,
Bungay, Suffolk.

ISBN 0 340 18629 1

This book is for
Richard

Sunday

FIRST DAY

I

A PIECE OF BROKEN GLASS CRUNCHED UNDER HIS FOOT as McKee moved to get a clearer view of the car. The Hillman Avenger had stopped at the far end of the runway and it seemed that the driving lesson was now over, for, through the Zeiss binoculars, McKee saw that the man had turned to face the girl. He watched a protective right arm encircle her shoulders, and then in a chain reaction their heads came together and they slid downward until they were almost out of sight.

Unlike McKee, the two boys crouching in the long grass at the foot of the derelict Control Tower were not even mildly interested in the occupants of the car. They were both just thirteen years old and the object of their attention was a one twenty-fourth scaled model of a Spitfire Mark II, which rose from the concrete runway and, responding to the signal from the transmitter, banked sharply to the right as soon as it became airborne. The buzz-saw whine of its tiny petrol-driven engine disturbed the quiet countryside and roused the couple in the Hillman Avenger.

The woman surfaced, brushed a strand of hair out of her eyes, fumbled with the ignition key and fired the car into life. Under her uncertain touch it hopped forward like a kangaroo and stalled. She did a little better at the second attempt and the car moved off smoothly. It came down the runway towards the Control Tower, swung right on to the taxiing circuit and disappeared from sight between the Spider Huts on the western edge of the airfield.

McKee crossed over to the opposite side of the briefing hut and focused on the car again as it approached the gap in the hedgerow bordering the minor road. He waited to see which direction it would take, knowing that the man and the woman would have to be exterminated if they chose the seclusion of the abandoned Officers' Mess which lay behind the clump of silver birch trees on the other side of the road. The prospect didn't worry him for there had been previous occasions when McKee had found it necessary to kill, but as it happened, the problem was resolved for him. The woman put the wheel over to the right and drove off towards Sutton-on-the-Forest, and McKee resumed his watch on the two boys.

He was particularly interested in the taller one, a boy with fair hair and freckled face called David Tarrant. There wasn't much McKee didn't know about David Tarrant, or his parents for that matter. He checked his watch, took one final look around the airfield to satisfy himself that there were no unwanted witnesses about and then strode out of the hut. He moved unhurriedly and made no attempt to conceal his approach.

It was some time before David Tarrant noticed the man walking towards them and even then he paid him little attention. He was endeavouring to put the Spitfire into an Immelmann turn and it would need all his concentration to effect the manoeuvre. James Stroud, his companion, had bet him tenpence that he couldn't do it. To avoid looking into the sun, he put the Spitfire through a one-hundred-and-eighty-degree turn and then sending it up into a steep climb, he waited for exactly the right moment before rolling it over and executing a perfect Immelmann. Flushed with success, he levelled out the diving aircraft and brought it in to land. Without a word being spoken, James Stroud handed over tenpence.

McKee said, 'That was really something.'

David Tarrant looked up into the dark eyes of the tall paratrooper standing in front of him. His glance took in the red beret, the combat suit with its disruptive pattern camouflage, the thick rubber-soled boots and the black polished gaiters. He noticed that the man was a Lieutenant-Colonel and carried a walking stick in his right hand.

'It was luck really,' he said quietly.

McKee smiled easily. 'If you say so,' he said. 'Personally, I think it was all skill.' He passed behind the boys. 'Don't let me disturb you,' he said, 'I'm just looking the place over to see if it would make a good DZ for my battalion.'

James Stroud said, 'Do you think I might have a go now?'

David Tarrant watched the paratrooper walk away and then turned his back on him. 'Yes, of course you can,' he said. 'Tell you what, if you can do an Immelmann you can have your money back.'

For a well-built man, McKee was very light on his feet, but then he had been trained to move with great stealth and he picked the right moment to strike. The noise of the tiny petrol engine masked the whoosh of the walking stick on its downward swing, and the nobbly end smashed into the base of James Stroud's skull. As his companion slumped over the control unit, David Tarrant turned his head sharply and took the full force of the second blow on his temple. Out of control now, the Spitfire bounced on to the runway, flipped over on to its back and caught fire. McKee dropped his walking stick, ran forward twenty yards and stamped out the blaze, smashing the model in the process.

As he kicked the wreckage into the long grass, McKee reached into his jacket pocket, brought out the Pye radio transmitter and erected its aerial. In a flat, emotionless voice, he spoke into the mouthpiece and said, 'This is Borodino, let's make the pick up now.' He waited for the brief acknowledgement, telescoped the aerial back into its socket and then slipped the radio into his jacket. McKee knew exactly where the boys had left their bicycles and he figured on hiding them in the disused Control Tower.

The long-wheelbase Land-Rover came out from behind the Officers' Mess, shot across the road and headed straight for the runway. It was driven by a short, ginger-haired Lance-Corporal; the name tag on his combat jacket was Silk. Seated beside him was another paratrooper named Goring and squashed up in the back of the vehicle along with two packing crates was a Private Findon. All three had been on edge, but now that the waiting was over, some of their tenseness and anxiety was slipping away.

Silk made directly for the tall figure standing beside the Control Tower and kept his speed down to fifty. It had been drummed into him that, although speed was essential, silence was paramount and McKee didn't want to hear any squealing tyres. Judging it well, Silk put the Land-Rover into a long, gentle, right-handed curve, eased off the accelerator pedal and touching the brakes lightly, brought the vehicle to a halt. He whipped it into reverse, backed up to the edge of the runway, braked, and then cut the engine.

They moved in concert because each man knew precisely what he had to do. Goring jumped out, ran to the back, let down the tailboard and with Findon's help, lifted the packing crates out and set them down on the grass. Silk walked over to the unconscious boys, and kneeling beside them, used his injection kits to give them a shot of Pentathol. Inside three minutes and in complete silence, they placed David Tarrant and James Stroud into the packing crates, replaced the lids and lifted them into the back of the Land-Rover. Findon scrambled in after them while Silk and Goring pushed the tailboard up and locked it into position, and then running to the front they tumbled into the vehicle. Almost leisurely, McKee strolled over and joined them.

He looked at Goring and said, 'This vehicle can take three up front; you'll have to sit with your legs astride the gear-box.' He waited until Goring was settled and then got in and closed the door.

Goring said, 'For Christ's sake, let's get out of here.'

McKee tapped his walking stick on the steel floor of the cab. 'Now listen to me, everybody,' he said firmly, 'there is absolutely no need to panic. We are four members of the 10th Parachute Battalion of the Territorial Army Volunteer Reserve, we are correctly dressed, we are displaying the correct Unit signs on our vehicle, and we will be keeping to side roads which are little used by the great motoring public, even if it is a Sunday. No one is going to give us a second glance.' He smiled reassuringly. 'All right,' he said, 'now let's move on.'

Their progress was a sedate forty-five miles an hour up through Stillington and Oswaldkirk and across to Ampleforth. Just before the village of Coxwold, they turned off the narrow country road and went up a lane which led to a disused gravel pit. Waiting for them farther up in the track in a natural bowl, were a Ford Zephyr towing a horse-box, a green-coloured Mini-Cooper and an Austin Maxi. Also waiting were two men and a woman.

The woman, Ruth Burroughs, was a blonde aged thirty-one, who had the sort of figure not usually associated with someone who spent most of her time around horses. She enjoyed dual nationality, and despite nine years in England, her voice still retained traces of an American accent. Her husband, twelve years her senior, looked almost old enough to be her father. Tall, thin, distinguished and balding, he gave the impression that he worked indoors; he was, in fact, a farmer. The last of the trio was Stephen Calvert, aged twenty-six, a salesman for Anglican Breweries.

The Land-Rover stopped abreast of them and McKee got out. Looking at Calvert, he said, 'You have our clothes?'

Calvert jerked his thumb in the direction of a clump of bushes. 'Over there,' he said, 'I thought you'd want some privacy.'

'Can you unload the crates and make the transfer while we change?'

Calvert smiled; nicotine had stained his teeth a dull yellow. 'I'm young, fit and healthy and I've got help. We'll manage.'

'See to it, then,' McKee said curtly. 'The taller of the two, the one with the freckles, goes into the boot of the Zephyr. The other is James Stroud; make sure you give him the Acid before you put him in the Maxi. When he comes round from the Pentathol, I want him to take off on a three-day trip. And when you've finished all that, I want the crates put back into the Land-Rover.' He turned and walked away; Goring, Findon and Silk followed him into the bushes.

Four suitcases were lined up in a row and in silence they stripped off their uniforms and changed into civilian clothes. The discarded combat suits, khaki shirts, berets, boots, anklets and web belts were packed away into the now empty suitcases which were then carried back to and placed inside the Land-Rover. The switch was completed in a time which would have been a credit to a troupe of quick-change artists.

McKee said, 'All right, we'll move off at two-minute intervals, Goring and Findon in the Mini, then Calvert and Silk in the Austin, followed by Ruth, Paul and myself in the Zephyr.'

Goring said, 'There's a little matter of an advance of our fee.'

'One hundred pounds each in used ten-, five- and one-pound notes—correct?'

'Yes.'

'The rest is waiting for you at the safe house.'

'We hope,' said Findon.

McKee said, 'You may rely on it. Give them their envelopes, Calvert, and get them out of here. I've got work to do.' He climbed into the Land-Rover and started the engine.

The lip of the gravel pit was another two hundred yards farther up the track and McKee didn't bother to shift out of first gear. He stopped the vehicle approximately thirty feet from the edge and walked forward to satisfy himself that the Land-Rover would have a clean drop into the water. It wasn't as sheer as McKee would have wished but there was no danger of the vehicle getting stuck on a protruding shelf when it went over. He returned to the Land-Rover, took off in first gear and then, once it was rolling, set the hand throttle and jumped out. There was no last-minute hitch except that the vehicle took rather longer to sink beneath the dark waters than McKee had expected.

Burroughs was sitting in the front of the Zephyr and had the engine ticking over. His fingers drummed a nervous tattoo on the steering wheel and he barely gave McKee time to close the rear door before he started moving.

Ruth said, 'You'll have to forgive my husband, waiting makes him nervous, and he's worried in case there aren't enough airholes in the boot.'

McKee ignored the comment; he knew the boy was in no danger of suffocating. 'You know the way?' he said to Burroughs.

'Of course, through Coxwold and then south on the A19.'

'Good. I see you've bought the horse, Ruth. Are you pleased with him?'

'I suppose so, but it wasn't the animal I was after.'

'Let's hope you won't be disappointed in him.'

'Why should you care?' said Burroughs. 'Thanks to you, our cover will be blown. I hope your friend is worth it.'

'He isn't my friend,' McKee said coldly, 'and I've never met him, but he's worth it all right.'

'What about Goring and Findon?'

'What about them?'

'They don't fit in.'

'Jarman hired them through a contractor.'

'My God,' said Burroughs, 'you must be out of your mind. They're just a couple of heavies and they probably have form. They'll betray us all if they're picked up.'

'They won't be, and Jarman will look after the contractor. Now pull off the road and let me have the box of tricks.'

Ruth Burroughs raised the lid of the central console between the front seats and took out an oblong-shaped radio some eight inches in length. 'Is this what you're looking for?' she said sweetly.

The green Mini-Cooper travelling east along the A170, overtook the Scammel and cut in sharply. Before the angry lorry-driver had time to flash his lights, the car disintegrated, and a millisecond later the blast wave shattered the windscreen in the cab of the truck. Half blinded by the flying glass, the Scammel driver swerved off the road and overturned in a ditch. Although most of the blast had travelled upwards, the force of the explosion had left a small crater in the road which went right down to the core. All that remained of Goring and Findon would scarcely have filled an average-sized dustbin.

2

THE PHOTOGRAPHS ON THE DRESSING-TABLE MOCKED him, and there were times when Tarrant was tempted to get rid of them, but somehow he never did. The wedding photograph was getting a little faded now but after fifteen years that was only to be expected. Everything and everybody changes with the years and that was certainly true of Alex and himself.

The photographer had caught them as they came out of the church under the archway of swords and Alex was laughing up at him. There had been a strong breeze and the wind had flattened the wedding dress against her breasts and long shapely legs, but her chestnut hair had stayed in place because she had worn it short in those days. He had been a lot thinner too, but of course he had been very young and his face was unlined then. It was a different story now and Tarrant didn't need to look in the mirror to see the web of fine lines under his eyes nor the deep crease marks on either side of his mouth to know that he had aged more than most over the years.

It was also a mistake to keep the portrait of David and Sarah, which had been taken in the living-room of their Quarter when they were both small and he was spending the year at the Staff College in Camberley. He had been very ambitious and hopeful in those days. Most of these days he felt a lot older than thirty-five and this was definitely one of them. Married at twenty, separated at thirty-two. Twelve years, with time out for separation when he had been stationed in Cyprus, Borneo and Aden, gone for nothing, because Alex couldn't stand it any longer, couldn't stand making the decisions when he wasn't there, couldn't stand being alone for month after month worrying about him and couldn't face him when he came home from Aden and learned how the girl had died.

It had been no one's fault. Sarah, coming home from school, had run across the main road without looking and a ten-ton Leyland had done the rest. There had been no need to cross the road at all, but it was a hot day and Sarah had told her friends that she fancied an ice-cream, and the sweet-shop was on the opposite side of the street. Tarrant had been flown home for the funeral, but when he returned to Aden, Alex had taken David and moved in with her parents.

They met from time to time at Speech Days, Exeats and end of term functions because David needed them both, but they were polite strangers. Twelve months after Sarah had been killed, Alex had found a flat in London and Tarrant had hopes that the umbilical cord had been severed. Her parents had never liked him, and divorced from their influence, he had thought there was a chance he might win her back. Three years later he was still nursing that hope.

He lived alone now in a tiny apartment on the eighth floor of a block of flats off Thessaly Road which gave him an unrivalled view of the Battersea Power Station and parts of Pimlico across the river. It was conveniently near the Main Building of the Ministry of Defence where he worked, and that was about all that could be said in its favour. He was a lonely man for whom work was an antidote, but this was Sunday and all Sundays were bloody.

The ringing of the telephone startled him out of his brooding and he went through to the sitting-room to answer it. It was, Tarrant thought, bound to be a wrong number; no one would call him on a Sunday evening. He was wrong, the caller was

Alex, and since she rarely phoned him, he sensed trouble. Without preamble, she said, 'John, a man has just phoned me about David.' There was a note of panic in her voice which alarmed Tarrant.

'What's happened to him?' he said tersely.

'I don't know. He just said that David was in trouble and only you could help him. He said he would phone again at seven-thirty and wanted to speak to you.'

Tarrant thought for a moment, and then said, 'Did he say what sort of trouble David was in?'

'If I knew that, I wouldn't be ringing you now.' Her voice had risen and it was shaky. Someone had really scared her and Alex was not the sort of person to be easily frightened. There was a whole string of questions which he wanted to ask her, but he knew that in her present state, he wouldn't get a coherent reply to any of them.

'All right,' he said, 'I'll be with you in thirty minutes.'

He had to wait for the lift and that set his nerves on edge, but he knew that if he ran down all eight flights he wouldn't save any time. He got the Zephyr out of the basement garage, cut across to Queenstown Road and went over the Chelsea Bridge. Alex had a flat in Chiswick with a view overlooking the park and Tarrant was beginning to think that he had been optimistic in thinking he could make it in half an hour.

He did it in less because the traffic was fairly light and he ignored the speed limit. He didn't have to ring, she was there on the doorstep waiting for him and she looked like death. He took her by the arm and led her into the flat, and he could see by the expression on her face that a whole torrent of anxious questions was about to pour out and that what Alex really wanted were comforting words to allay her fears.

Tarrant said, 'Who else have you phoned apart from me?'

'The school,' she whispered. 'I spoke to the Matron because the Housemaster was over in the Gym coaching the fencing team. She told me that David had booked out for the afternoon. He and another boy have gone on their bikes to Sutton-on-the-

Forest.' She blinked her eyes rapidly. 'He's had an accident,' she said, 'I know he has.'

'You'd have heard from the police by now if he had.' Tarrant picked up the telephone and began dialling.

'Who are you calling?' she said.

'The school, I want to speak to someone in authority.' Her teeth were nibbling at a thumbnail and he knew that he had to give her something to do to take her mind off David.

'You can't do anything here,' he said firmly, 'so why not go into the kitchen and make a pot of tea. We could both use a cup.' He turned his back on her, cutting short any protest.

A voice in his ear said, 'Quinton House.'

'Oh, good evening, Mr Dyson,' he said, 'this is John Tarrant. Just about an hour ago, my wife had a very strange telephone call from someone not connected with the school, saying that David was in trouble. I understand that Matron told Alex that David and another boy had gone to Sutton-on-the-Forest and I wondered if they had returned yet?' He listened intently and then said, 'It may not be anything serious, but if he isn't back by seven, would you please call me immediately at 01-108-9984.' He listened again, thanked Dyson and then hung up. Looking round, he saw Alex standing in the doorway.

'What did he have to say?' she said.

'David and James Stroud went off together but Mr Dyson doesn't think there is anything to worry about and he'll call me as soon as they return. They've got to be back for Chapel at seven anyway.' He walked across the room and placed both hands on her shoulders. 'Look,' he said quietly, 'I don't think there's anything to worry about either. The phone call was probably a hoax.'

'Why would anyone do a thing like that?'

'I don't know, I honestly don't know, it would be a pretty sick kind of a joke.'

'You don't seem sure?'

'David is all right, I'm sure of that, and if it is a hoaxer—well, I'll be here to blast him off the other end of the phone.' He smiled, and in a quieter voice, said, 'I could use that cup of tea now.'

She hesitated and then turned away and went into the kitchen again.

He had a very clear picture of the deserted airfield at Sutton-on-the-Forest and there were any number of places where a boy could get into trouble if he was careless. The old air-raid shelters and the Control Tower were potential hazards, but he couldn't see David falling into or off either of them, and in any case, the message Alex had received tended to rule out the possibility that he had been injured. It might be that an irate farmer had caught them trespassing on his land, but it was scarcely likely that he would think of detaining them. If they had done any damage, a reasonable man would take their names and addresses and then call their parents.

Alex said, 'Here's your cup of tea.' She placed it on the coffee table in front of the couch.

Tarrant said, 'I've been thinking; perhaps a farmer caught them trespassing on his land.'

Her face brightened visibly. 'Do you really think so?'

'Well, there's one way of finding out, we could phone the Strouds and ask them if they too have had a telephone call. Do you know their address?'

'No, I don't.'

'Do you know where they live?'

'Leeds, I think, or is it Wakefield?'

'I'll call Dyson,' said Tarrant, 'he'll have their number if they are on the phone.'

Dyson answered his call and anticipated the wrong question.

He said, 'I'm afraid they haven't returned yet, Major Tarrant, but of course there's still some time to go before Chapel.' There was a note of disquiet in his voice. 'However, I have been on to the North Riding Police, but they've had no report of an accident involving two boys.'

Tarrant said, 'As a matter of fact, I think we can rule out the possibility of an accident. I believe they might have been caught trespassing on someone's property.'

'I very much doubt if that is the case, Major Tarrant. They go to the airfield every Sunday to fly David's Spitfire, and we've never had a complaint about their behaviour before.'

'Perhaps the radio control packed up and the plane strayed on to the adjoining farmland. You never know, it could have crashed into a greenhouse or something like that.'

There was a longish pause and then Dyson said, 'I hadn't considered that possibility.'

'I thought I'd ring the Strouds and see if they'd had a complaint too. Do you happen to know their number?'

'I think it would be best if I spoke to them, Major Tarrant,' Dyson said coolly, 'we don't want to alarm them unnecessarily. I'll phone you back immediately after I have been in touch with them.' He rang off before Tarrant had a chance to object.

'I knew you shouldn't have bought him that bloody Spitfire for Christmas,' Alex said vehemently. 'I'll never forgive you if anything has happened to him.'

Tarrant drank his cup of tea; it was lukewarm. 'Don't let's anticipate bad news,' he said, 'we don't know for certain that anything has happened to him.'

'He wouldn't have gone to Sutton-on-the-Forest if you hadn't given him that damn model to play with.'

'He's been going there for weeks and nothing has happened to him.'

'Don't shout at me.'

'I'm not shouting.' He walked over to the sideboard, poured out two whiskies, added a splash of soda and gave one glass to Alex. 'Here,' he said, 'drink this, you'll feel better.' Tears gathered in her eyes and rolled down her cheeks. 'Nothing's happened to David, has it? I couldn't bear it if . . .' He took the glass out of her hand and placed it on the table with his, and then he put his arms around her. She buried her face in his chest and he could feel her shoulders shaking as she cried into his shirt front.

'It's going to be all right,' he said lamely, 'you see if it isn't.

Now, come on, try and keep your chin up.' The words sounded trite and banal but he couldn't think of anything else to say. He kept glancing at the clock on the mantelpiece and willing Dyson to ring back. They had to wait long, drawn-out minutes before they heard from him.

Dyson said, 'I'm afraid I can't get in touch with the Strouds, they're not answering their phone. Perhaps they've gone away for the weekend.'

'Never mind about the Strouds, what about my son?'

'David and James still haven't returned.'

Tarrant said, 'You'd better get on to the police again, Mr Dyson.'

'I already have. They're sending a car out to the airfield. I'll call you as soon as I hear from them.'

Tarrant replaced the receiver slowly and turned to face Alex. She was sitting hunched up on the sofa as if she was cold. Her eyes were red and puffy and the glass of whisky trembled in her hand.

'What do you think has happened to him?' she said huskily.

Tarrant lit a cigarette. 'They've probably decided to cut Chapel,' he said savagely, 'and we're sitting here stewing our insides out.'

'Perhaps he's been kidnapped?'

'Don't be stupid.'

'It happens. Babies are often taken from their prams.'

'He's no baby, he's thirteen, and there's another boy with him. Can you see anybody trying to snatch two thirteen-year-olds?'

'He's only a child, John,' she snapped, 'he's not a grown man who can defend himself.'

Tarrant stubbed out his cigarette and poured himself another whisky. 'Put that idea out of your head,' he said quietly, 'you're making yourself ill.'

'I can't,' she said, 'you wouldn't understand. I'm his mother.'

'And I'm his father.'

'Then try acting like one.'

Tarrant bit back a retort; a slanging match was the last thing he wanted. He watched the clock as if his life depended on it.

The telephone rang promptly at seven-thirty and he snatched up the receiver.

The voice was calm, almost soothing. It said, 'My name is Drabble. We haven't had the pleasure of meeting one another, Major Tarrant, but I feel I know you very well. I believe you have a son called David.'

'What is this ... ?'

'He's at a boarding school in York, and your father-in-law, who is a Bradford wool merchant, pays the school fees.'

'What are you trying to tell me?' Tarrant said angrily.

'He has a friend called James Stroud, and every Sunday for the past few weeks, they have been riding out to Sutton-on-the-Forest where David flies his model Spitfire.'

'For God's sake, what has happened to him?'

'He's in my care, Major Tarrant.'

'I'm not sure I understand.'

'You might say he's been kidnapped.'

'Oh Christ. Why? I haven't got any money. How do we get him back?'

'Well, I'd rather like to know what action you've taken so far?'

'I've rung David's Housemaster and he has been in touch with the local police.'

'That's very satisfactory. I don't think you need bother to tell anyone else at this stage. Now listen carefully. I want you to return to your flat where you will find an envelope waiting for you. Inside the envelope you will find a key to a left luggage compartment in St Pancras Station. The number of the compartment is thirty-six—have you got that?'

'Yes.'

'Good. There is a letter waiting for you at St Pancras which will tell you what you have to do.'

Tarrant licked his lips. 'How do I know you've got my son?' he said quietly.

'I thought you might ask me that question. Perhaps this will put your mind at rest.'

Tarrant heard the spool hissing on the tape recorder, and then David started speaking, and the boy was badly frightened because his voice was high-pitched and unsteady, and he was saying that they weren't to worry but would they please do what Mr Drabble wanted. And Alex could hear every word because she was standing at Tarrant's shoulder and the tape recorder was running at maximum volume, and then the brief message ended in a long-sustained hiss and Alex tore the phone out of his hand.

'I'll kill you,' she screamed. 'I'll kill you if you lay a finger on him.'

The threat didn't excite Drabble, he sounded bored. Tarrant heard him say, 'Would you please get your wife off the line, we still have business to do.'

Tarrant prised the phone out of her grasp. 'All right,' he said loudly, 'what do you want now?'

Drabble said, 'I shall be telephoning your wife again tomorrow evening at ten past eight and I want to speak to someone in authority.'

'Who?'

'You'll know who,' said Drabble.

The Swiftsure Detective Agency was in Long Acre across the road from the Talk of the Town. Sandwiched between a bookshop and a philatelist's, it was on the first landing with Troy Fashions (Ladies' Lingerie) beneath, and a call-girl operating under the name of Gina—Secretarial Services, on the floor above. Worn linoleum covered the floor of the office and the walls needed distempering, but the steel desk, steel filing cabinet and tubular steel chairs looked new. Propped on the windowsill behind the desk, were copies of the *Trade Directory*, *Whittaker's Almanac*, *Debrett*, The Army Gradation List, the Navy and Air Force Lists, *Who's Who* and *Kelly's Handbook* 1968 edition. The Swiftsure Detective Agency sounded big, but it consisted of just one operative, a man called Penfold, and it was difficult to see why he needed to be so well-informed about the Armed Services and the Peerage.

Penfold was a plump, shabby-looking man in his early forties. Frayed shirt cuffs showed below the sleeves of his blue pin-stripe, dandruff speckled the lapels of his jacket, and there were food stains on his waistcoat. He was something of a character actor, for the Agency was merely an elaborate front for his other activities. Penfold was The Contractor.

Normally, he would not have come into the office late on a Sunday evening, but he was there to meet Crosby who had been very insistent that the matter was urgent. He had smoked several cigarettes, and he was beginning to get a little tired of waiting for Crosby to show up, when a soft tapping noise brought him to his feet and he walked across the office and opened the door.

'Oh, it's you,' he said sourly, 'it's about time. You'd better come inside.' He turned his back on Crosby, and that was a fatal error. The door clicked behind him and then the edge of Crosby's right hand scythed into the back of his neck and broke it as easily as if it were a piece of fragile bone china. With almost catlike reflexes, Crosby caught hold of Penfold's body and lowered it gently on to the floor. He then switched out the lights and stood there in the quiet office listening intently. He heard the patter of urgent feet on the staircase and waited. Somewhere above a radio was playing.

Crosby allowed five minutes to pass before he crept out of the office and locked the door behind him. As he was about to leave, some instinct made him look up, and on the landing above he saw a girl in profile, and at that precise moment, she also turned her head and noticed him. Knee-length blue suede boots hugged her silken legs, red satin hot-pants strained against her hips and the white blouse was slashed in a deep V.

'What are you waiting down there for?' she said. 'I'm Gina, I won't eat you.' Her voice was harsh and beginning to rise. 'Well, make up your mind,' she snapped, 'I haven't got all night.' If he backed away, there was always a chance that she might follow him down to the street mouthing abuse; he climbed the few steps to the upper landing.

She smiled without warmth. 'That's better. For a moment I thought we'd have to get the dog to bring you in.' There was another open door to his right and, as he glanced sideways, his eyes met a contemptuous sneer. The woman was over fifty, stout, and wore a shapeless dress over her lumpy figure. Grey hair resembled a raveged bird's nest, the stockings hung in wrinkles around her fat legs and swollen ankles and her toes were poking out of the carpet slippers. The Alsatian lying at her feet raised its head and snarled at him. Something foul was simmering on the stove; it smelt like boiled cabbage.

Gina said, 'That's Hilda, my maid; she'll see we're not disturbed.' Hilda favoured Crosby with another sneer. He followed Gina into the bedroom and noticed that she was limping slightly.

'Take your jacket off and make yourself comfortable,' she said. She sat down on the bed, crossed her legs and casually lit a cigarette; pink lipstick formed a tide-mark around the filter tip. 'My fee is three pounds and a tip for the maid,' she said flatly.

Crosby weighed up the alternatives. He had been pushed into taking an enormous risk, but his life was always a series of risks, and there was no other real option open to him. It wouldn't take long, and theirs was always a mechanical performance, and the chances were that she wouldn't remember him, and Penfold was lying dead inside a dark locked office where no one could see him, and in less than two hours he would be catching the night flight to Paris. And with these factors in mind, he took a five-pound note out of his wallet and laid it on the bedside table.

Like an animated wooden doll, she stubbed out her cigarette in the ashtray, unzipped the hot-pants and stepped out of them, and then she rolled the tights down to her ankles.

Crosby said, 'What about my change?'

She raised her head and forced a bright smile on to her face. 'Listen,' she said, 'for five pounds I can show you some interesting variations. The French have a certain way of doing things.'

The man called Crosby, whom McKee knew as Jarman, allowed her to show him.

The instructions in Drabble's letter were quite explicit and Tarrant wasted little time before telephoning Colonel Robin Mulholland. Officers like Tarrant, who worked in Military Intelligence, were expected to know where they could reach their Commanding Officer in out of duty hours. Drabble wanted to talk to the Director of Subversive Warfare whose name was Harper, and while this man was not exactly a stranger to Tarrant, he felt it would be best if Mulholland spoke to him first.

Monday

SECOND DAY

3

THE WINDOW, A DIRT-STAINED PORTHOLE ABOUT FIVE feet in diameter, was divided by strips of wood into a number of octagonal segments. Pigeons roosted on the ledge outside and left their droppings on the glass. A firm of contractors gave the building a face-lift every three years, and it was said that, after they had washed the grime off the windows, you could actually see the National Gallery across the square. Winter or summer, strip lighting was constantly used in Harper's office.

Harper was a man of average height and build, quiet yet authoritative, but saddled with a streak of obstinacy; a man, who once he had made up his mind that he was in the right, would not be deflected by argument. Those who knew him best said that he was very much a family man with wide-ranging interests outside his job, but if this was so, he took great care to conceal it from his colleagues. Outwardly then, he was a youthful-looking forty-eight with brown hair parted neatly on the left side, brown eyes and an unlined face in which the mouth seemed permanently on the point of breaking out into a smile.

In the few months that they had been acquainted, Mulholland had come to realise that it was a mistake to judge Harper superficially.

Harper said, 'I don't see why Major Tarrant has to see me.'

'But you were specifically named in the letter he received.'

'And my Department.'

It was more a statement of fact than a question, but Mulholland felt a reply of some kind was expected. 'And your Department,' he agreed reluctantly.

'Tell me, in your opinion, how many people know of the Department for Subversive Warfare?'

Mulholland shifted uncomfortably in his chair. 'Everyone who attends the weekly meeting of the General Purpose Intelligence Committee.'

'Which, of course, includes Tarrant.'

'Amongst many others,' Mulholland said defensively. 'Don't forget that the Press is also aware that such an organisation does exist.'

'Quite. But few outside Whitehall are as conversant with its detailed organisation as the writer of this letter seems to be. Could it be a hoax?'

'The kidnapping?'

'What else?'

'The police have confirmed that two schoolboys are definitely missing. It was on the news this morning.'

'I didn't hear it.'

'I did.'

'What's your opinion of Tarrant?'

'You've seen him at the committee meetings.'

'That isn't what I meant.'

Mulholland smoothed the thinning blond hair across his pink scalp; it was a habit of his when embarrassed. 'Well, he's thirty-five, he was born in London of—shall we say, lower-middle-class parents—he attended a Direct Grant Grammar School as a day boy, got three A levels and entered Sandhurst at eighteen. He married the only daughter of a Yorkshire wool merchant when he was twenty but separated from her three years ago. He lives alone in a flat off Thessaly Road, and there is no girl-friend that I know of.'

Harper placed the letter on his blotter. 'You're a bit of a snob, Mulholland,' he said casually.

'I don't think I am,' Mulholland said heatedly. 'Tarrant's a good man, he won a Military Cross in Aden and only recently he was Positively Vetted.'

'That practically makes him a saint.'

'Will you see him now?'

'Yes.'

'Do you want me to stay on?'

Harper examined his fingernails. 'I don't think that will be necessary,' he said quietly.

Mulholland was a cavalry officer, and perhaps the saddest aspect of his life was the fact that he would never serve with his regiment again. The red tabs of a Colonel on the General Staff was a poor consolation. He didn't mind working in Military Intelligence but he could strike no rapport with men like Harper, whose agency was outside the jurisdiction of the Ministry of Defence, and he doubted if Tarrant would either.

In this he was wrong. Harper was at pains to put Tarrant at his ease.

He said, 'I don't think you've ever been inside my office before, Major Tarrant. I'm afraid it's rather a poky little place. Do please sit down.' He pushed the carved cigarette box across the desk. 'I don't use them myself but perhaps you would care for one?' Tarrant helped himself and leaned forward to catch the flame from Harper's gold Dunhill.

'You look tired.'

'I hardly slept at all last night.'

'No, I don't suppose you did.' Harper picked up the sheet of paper. 'Of course I've read this letter you collected from the left luggage at St Pancras, but there are one or two questions I'd like to ask you.'

'I understand.'

'Are you a rich man, Major Tarrant?'

'What?'

'Your son has been kidnapped, so whoever did it must have some asking price in mind.'

'I haven't got a private income.'

'How about your father-in-law?'

'He's fairly comfortably off but I wouldn't describe him as a wealthy man.'

'And I don't suppose your parents would be in a position to help you?' Harper said diplomatically.

'They're both dead.'

Harper dropped the letter on to the desk. 'Your son wasn't alone when he was kidnapped?'

'No, there was a boy called James Stroud with him, and he's still missing.'

'Has this man Drabble contacted Stroud's parents?'

'No. At least he hadn't before I left home this morning.'

'How odd. Of course, you reported the kidnapping to the Metropolitan Police?'

'Yes, after I collected the letter.'

'Why not before?'

'The North Riding Police were already looking for them. I thought it was more important to see what was in the letter.'

'Why do you think this man Drabble wants to speak to me?'

'I really don't know.'

'Is anyone with your wife at the moment? Her mother perhaps?'

'No, she's alone. Her mother wanted to come down from Bradford last night, but you see, she's very fond of her grandson, and quite honestly, she's not very much good in a crisis, and Alex thought she would only make things worse.'

'Have there been other crises?'

'Our daughter was killed in a traffic accident four years ago.'

'I'm sorry. Was that the cause of your separation?'

Tarrant could feel the colour flowing into his face. 'There were other reasons,' he said quietly. 'Sarah's death was the final straw.'

Harper said smoothly, 'I apologise, I didn't mean to pry into your private life.' He picked up a pencil and drew a number of circles on the blotting-paper. 'I shouldn't think for a minute that Colonel Mulholland will expect to see you in the office again until this affair is over. Where can I get in touch with you should the need arise?'

'At my wife's flat,' and then for no reason he felt compelled to say, 'there's a spare bedroom.'

Harper raised an eyebrow. 'Oh yes?' he said vaguely.

Tarrant said hesitantly, 'Will you be there tonight, sir, when Drabble phones?'

'Of course I will. Could I have the address?'

'26B, Niger Avenue, Chiswick.'

Harper wrote it down on his pad, looked up and smiled. 'I'll be there just before eight,' he said. Tarrant thanked him, stubbed out his cigarette and left. It wasn't until he was walking down Whitehall that he remembered Harper still had Drabble's letter.

Harper was a man with a logical mind who liked to think a problem out, and Tarrant was most definitely a problem, and the trouble was that he didn't know enough about the man. There was little point in approaching MI5 to see what they had on him because Tarrant had only recently been positively vetted, but if there was anything shady about his private life which had been missed, then Special Branch were just the people to sniff it out.

He pressed the button on the office intercom and said, 'Miss Nightingale, would you please get me Chief Superintendent Wray on the green line?' Miss Nightingale was extremely efficient; he was connected in less than two minutes.

A gruff voice said, 'Good morning, Cedric, what can I do for you?'

'A lot, I hope,' said Harper, 'but I think we had better switch to secure means. Will you press your scrambler button now please?' He waited for a few moments and then said, 'Stanley, I have a problem with a young army officer called Tarrant whose son has apparently been kidnapped. Now I know kidnapping is outside your province, but I would like to know a lot more about his background than I do at present. You see, he's with Military Intelligence and his section deals with Russia and the Warsaw Pact countries. I think we ought to have lunch together—say one o'clock at my club, if that's convenient?'

Wray said that it was.

The branch line to Barnard Castle had been closed for years. Rails and sleepers had been ripped up and the gravel chippings had disappeared beneath the encroaching grass. Indeed, except for the obvious cuttings and embankments, it was not easy now to see exactly where the permanent way had been.

At ten that morning, a group of sixth-formers from the Russell Turner Comprehensive began walking the line from Barnard Castle to Darlington, mapping the old railway route as part of a school project. They had been going for nearly two hours and were well out into the country when they came across the boy. He was weaving towards them, and as far as they could deduce from his almost incoherent speech, he said his name was James Stroud and he had been sleeping in an old plate-layer's hut. Despite his obvious youth, they were under the impression that he was drunk until one of their number spotted the egg-shaped lump and dried blood in the hair at the base of his skull. Convinced then that he was suffering from concussion, they insisted on carrying him to the main road by the most direct cross country route, while the fastest runner went ahead to phone for an ambulance.

At a quarter past one, James Stroud was admitted to the County Hospital, where a clinical examination showed that he was suffering from a mild case of concussion. Further tests revealed that he had been given Lysergic Acid Diethylamide. A request by the police to take a statement from him was refused on the grounds that he was still under the influence of the drug.

McKee had always admired the dining-room because it had a

touch of grandeur about it. He liked the mullioned bow windows, the Spanish mahogany dining-table and chairs and the deep pile carpet which toned with the velvet drapes. The Burroughs knew how to live in style but of course they had had a head start with their converted Georgian farmhouse.

He pushed back his chair and stretching out his legs, crossed them at the ankle. 'I liked the wine, Paul,' he said, 'you have quite a cellar.'

'It's getting a little crowded,' Burroughs said pointedly.

'We had to put the boy somewhere. I thought it was an ideal spot—soundproof, secure and adequately ventilated—what more could you ask?'

'For you to go away.'

The smile faded on McKee's face. 'I'm afraid that's impossible,' he said softly.

'Then I only hope what we are doing is worth it.'

'I really am getting rather bored with that line, Paul.'

'Killing Findon and Goring was a mistake.'

'You think so?' McKee said icily.

'You know damn well it was, and dumping the Stroud boy was another.'

'The people we shall be dealing with are a very hard-headed lot and we shall really have to frighten them to show that we mean business. Now, it would be bad for public relations if we'd killed the other boy, but Goring and Findon are in a different category. Their death is a sort of curtain-raiser.'

Burroughs stood up. 'If you'll excuse me,' he said shakily, 'it's nearly two o'clock and I've got work to do.'

'Don't tell me—you've got a farm to run.'

'But only for a few more days.' The heavy footsteps and the door slamming behind Burroughs were obvious signs of his bitterness, anger and fear.

McKee said, 'I'm sure you want to add your piece, Ruth.'

Ruth Burroughs smiled. 'You mustn't take it to heart; Paul is naturally disappointed to be leaving this place after he has made such a success of it.'

'With our help, don't forget.'

'With your help,' she agreed, 'but things have been getting on top of him.' A slim hand strayed across the table and lightly touched his wrist. 'You understand?'

'What's he worried about? Around here he is known to be a Radio Ham. He has sent his last official message so now he can just amuse himself talking to that schoolteacher friend of his in Johore Bahru.'

Her eyes were deep and watchful. 'Sometimes I wonder about you,' she said quietly. 'Are you a lonely man?'

'As lonely as Tarrant.'

'You're alike?'

'As brothers,' he said morosely, 'but not in appearance. He's taller, heavier and fair, and of course he's ten years younger, but we have a lot in common—an over-riding sense of loyalty, amongst other things. In a way, it's a pity we have to destroy him.'

They were like strangers at a party, sizing one another up while they made small talk. Wray was hardly a social asset but then it was hardly a social occasion. He was a medium-sized man with iron-grey hair and a weight problem. Exchanging pleasantries was not his forte.

The lounge in Alex's flat had undergone a drastic change, and now it was more like an Operations Centre than a home. A Grundig tape recorder had been plugged into the domestic telephone, and a second phone, giving them a direct line to the GPO Tower, had just been installed. This latter one was permanently manned by a duty policeman, who would be changed every eight hours round the clock.

There were five of them—Harper, Wray, Alex, Tarrant and the duty policeman—and their eyes were on the domestic telephone willing it to ring. In such a tense atmosphere the conversation was bound to be limited. At exactly ten minutes past eight the phone began to ring.

Tarrant answered it and said, '9984.'

Drabble said, 'Is Mr Harper there?'

'You want to speak to him?'

'Naturally; would you put him on the line?'

Harper took the phone out of Tarrant's hand. 'I'm listening,' he said, 'what do you want?'

'Yesterday, a Mini travelling east along the A 170, was blown up by a bomb. According to the papers, the police seem to think the IRA had a hand in it . . .'

Harper said, 'The line must be bad, you keep fading away. Would you start again?' By needling Drabble and prolonging the conversation, Harper was trying to give the GPO enough time to trace the call. On STD that would not be easy.

Drabble said, 'That's the last time you'll interrupt me unless you want the boy to suffer. If you miss anything, you can always play it back.'

'Why should you think this conversation is being taped?'

'Because you would be incompetent if it wasn't. Those two men in the car—I want you to know that we killed them with fifty pounds of plastic explosive moulded into the frame of both front seats which we detonated by transmitting a command signal by radio. Think about that while you wait for me to call again.'

Harper started to say something and then realised that Drabble had ended the conversation. He looked at Wray and said, 'What do you think?'

'He's trying to frighten us, and I don't believe he killed those two men, but I have to admit that if he gave us their names, I'd be forced to revise my opinion.'

Tarrant said, 'We're frightened enough already; you seem to forget that he has our son.'

It was but a gentle rebuke, but it went home, and it fell to the duty policeman to break the embarrassed silence. He cleared his throat and said, 'I'm afraid the GPO didn't have time to trace the call, sir. They think it came from somewhere in the Northampton area.'

No one took him up on it but the inference was plain. They

would have to do better when Drabble contacted them again.

The phone rang at 8:25 pm and Harper answered it.

Drabble said, 'We want five hundred thousand pounds. Tarrant doesn't have that kind of money and his father-in-law would be pushed to raise half that amount, but you can, Harper, you can raise it easily.'

Harper said, 'Just a minute—you're not the same man I spoke to a quarter of an hour ago.'

The laughter came over clearly and then the voice said, 'There's more than one Drabble, Harper.'

There were two of them, and they spoke alternately and at irregular intervals and they defeated every attempt Harper made to hold the line open.

At 8:37 pm, Drabble said, 'We want the money in uncut diamonds. You will purchase them from Rand and Goodbody and you will obtain a bill of sale.'

At 8:40 pm, the message continued, 'I will contact you again tomorrow at this number at 7:15 pm to instruct you where to send the bill of sale.'

At 9:18 pm, 'Keep the Press out of this, they will only complicate matters—play down any idea that David Tarrant has been kidnapped and think up a cover story to explain the reappearance of the Stroud boy.'

The final message was timed at 9:31 pm. Drabble said, 'You may think we are bluffing; perhaps this recording will help to dispel that illusion.'

The tape hissed, and then David said edgily, 'I could make that plane do almost anything, really I could, Mr Drabble.'

'What sort of plane was it, David?'

'You're not really interested.'

'Oh, but I am.'

'It was a Spitf ... a-a-a-a-a-a-ah.'

The scream was going to live with Tarrant for the rest of his life and he thought he was going to be sick.

Drabble said, 'We burnt his neck with a cigarette end, and we'll keep on burning him until we get what we want.' There was a dull clunk as he hung up.

Harper slowly replaced the receiver and said nothing. There was nothing he could say. His eyes were on Alex Tarrant and he could see that she was shaking like a leaf, and then she started to retch and her hand flew to her mouth to hold back the vomit in her throat. She struggled to her feet and ran out of the room; Tarrant looked questioningly at Harper and then followed her.

Wray said, 'Someone seems to know the size of your budget, Cedric.'

'Someone seems to know a damn sight too much about me,' Harper snapped. 'I don't think there is any point staying here any longer. Can you give me a lift to Waterloo?'

'Will you see Tarrant before you leave?'

'Certainly.'

'And?'

'And I'll tell him that the Department will furnish a bill of sale. If we have to, we'll even put up the money.'

It was a warm muggy night and the rumble of thunder in the distance heralded the approaching storm. Scattered raindrops splashed against the windscreen of Wray's car as they drove in silence. They had reached Victoria Street before Harper voiced his thoughts.

He said, 'If I was going to kidnap a child, I'd make sure the parents could pay the ransom.'

Wray said, 'I'd go along with that.'

'And yet they deliberately chose David Tarrant and named me to put up the money.'

'Well?'

'Well, Jesus Christ, Stanley, you don't think they got my name out of the Yellow Pages, do you?'

'What are you leading up to?'

'I want you to put Tarrant under close surveillance as soon as possible.'

Tuesday

THIRD DAY

4

A CRICK IN THE NECK, WHERE HIS HEAD HAD BEEN LYING awkwardly across the arm of the sofa, woke Tarrant up just as it was getting light. He shifted into a more comfortable position and tried to go back to sleep, but the duty policeman, who occupied a camp-bed just inside the door, was snoring loudly and the noise kept him awake. It would have been more convenient if Tarrant had slept in David's room, but for some inexplicable reason he felt that that would be wrong, and, in the circumstances, he could hardly share a bed with Alex. It was his second night on the couch and the lack of sleep was slowly having its effect.

A milk float whirred along the road and stopped outside the flat, urgent feet took the steps two at a time, milk bottles clinked one against the other, and then, whistling cheerfully, the milkman returned to the float and drove off. Five minutes later, a bicycle scraped against the kerb, the letter-box clattered and the newspaper plopped on to the mat in the hall. He lay there for a while and then reluctantly came to the conclusion that his brain was now too active to allow him any further rest.

He slid off the couch, padded across the room and, carefully avoiding the recumbent figure on the camp-bed, opened the door and stepped out into the hall. He collected the paper and then went through to the kitchen to make the early morning tea.

He smoked a couple of cigarettes while he read the *Daily Telegraph* from cover to cover. There was a small paragraph on page four describing how James Stroud had been discovered wandering along the old railway line between Barnard Castle and Darlington and which ended with the observation that the search was still continuing for the other missing boy.

At eight, he woke Alex with a cup of tea and then went into the lounge to draw the curtains, only to find that the job had been done for him. He opened a side window and he could smell the freshess of the rain-washed grass in the park across the road. He paid little attention to the man sitting in the Vauxhall Viva outside the park gates.

The car was there for a definite purpose, and it mattered little whether Tarrant appreciated its significance or not. In the circumstances, it would be routine procedure to keep the street under surveillance in case the opposition were also watching the flat to see how the Tarrants were reacting, but in this instance, the police were more intersted in Tarrant than they were in anyone else.

The man from Special Branch parked his car in the basement garage of the tower block off Thessaly Road and then took the lift up to the eighth floor. He walked boldly along the corridor and, using a piece of mica, opened the door of Tarrant's flat and slipped inside the hall. Even if he had met anyone in the corridor, his presence inside the building would not have been questioned; he was dressed in the uniform of the South-Eastern Electricity Board, and the casual observer would presume that he had come to read the meters.

Chief Superintendent Wray's briefing had been necessarily vague, but Chesterman was an experienced agent who had worked on the Lonsdale case, and he knew what to look for. He went through the flat with a fine toothcomb, starting with the bedroom where he rifled through the clothes hanging up in the wardrobe and turning over the contents of the chest of drawers. Before leaving the room, he sounded the walls, but despite his systematic and painstaking approach, he could find no trace of a cavity. He repeated the process with the small dining-room, kitchen, sitting-room and bathroom with equally negative results. He also checked the cistern and the hot-water tanks with the same thoroughness.

Chesterman worked unhurriedly, secure in the knowledge that he would not be disturbed, because the man in the Vauxhall Viva would take care of that problem. If Tarrant left his wife's flat in Chiswick, Chesterman would be warned in minutes by telephone. He left the writing desk until last, but even here, he found nothing untoward. From the bills, bank statements, old letters and snapshots, Chesterman formed the impression that they were dealing with a very ordinary man who, apparently, had little to hide. He noted that Tarrant possessed a Japanese 'Hit Parade' tape recorder and a number of cassettes embracing a wide range of taste in music from Tchaikovsky to Kenny Ball. There was also an old, rather battered Empire Aristocrat portable typewriter.

He found a sheet of foolscap in the bottom drawer of the desk, fed it into the machine and then, four-finger, two-thumb style, typed, 'Now is the time for all good men to come to the aid of the party.' He moved the line space lever, typed the phrase again, removed the foolscap, folded it in half and half again and then placed it inside his wallet. As a final gesture, he picked up the telephone, removed the base-plate, looked inside and found a metal surface to which the magnetised bug would adhere. He then reassembled the phone and left the flat.

Chesterman took the lift back down to the basement garage and, walking across to his car, opened the boot and took out a grip. He carried it with him into the lavatories and found a vacant cubicle where he changed his clothes. Ten minutes later he reappeared dressed in a dark mohair suit, got into the car and drove up to street level. He followed a circular route which took in Battersea Park Road, Nine Elms Lane and South Lambeth Road before returning to the tower block, where he found a vacant parking space in the forecourt facing the main entrance.

He locked the car, crossed the pavement, went through the swing doors and sought out the caretaker in his office.

Chesterman took an instant dislike to the man. The caretaker was suspicious, belligerent, ingratiating and co-operative in turn: suspicious on meeting a stranger, belligerent when Chesterman informed him that he was making enquiries on behalf of a firm of solicitors, ingratiating when he saw a pound note waving under his nose and co-operative when he got his hands on the money, in the hope that there would be more where that came from.

Chesterman said, 'This client of ours is anxious to divorce his wife and although we've got the name of one co-respondent, we'd like a few more.' Chesterman winked. 'This client,' he said, 'hasn't exactly been a monk himself and he's anxious not to pay any more maintenance than he has to. We've heard his wife has been playing around with a Major Tarrant.'

'Bloke on the eighth floor?'

'Yes; know anything about him?'

'Keeps himself pretty much to himself, mister.'

Chesterman showed him another pound note. 'But not always?' he suggested.

'Once he had a bird stay the night.'

'Oh?'

'Almost five months ago—must have been New Year's Day—she was still wearing this evening dress when I seen them get out of the lift—it would be about half past eight in the morning because I'd just clocked in.'

'What was she like?'

'Good-looking tart, about thirty, a redhead.' He leered into Chesterman's face. 'I wouldn't have minded her touching me up, mate,' he said.

Chesterman managed to hide his repugnance. 'Did he mention her name?'

'Huh?'

'Well, you know—did he say something like, I'll see you again Alice?'

'It wasn't Alice—he called her Barbara—said he'd see her at lunch as usual.'

Chesterman tucked the note into the caretaker's shirt pocket. 'Here,' he said, 'buy yourself a drink; better still, go out and get stoned, you deserve it.'

Even though the job description put it differently, Calvert was essentially a travelling man. He covered the Home Counties for Anglican Breweries and his movements were entirely predictable to the extent that McKee knew just where to find him. Tuesdays were set aside for East Kent, and Calvert always lunched at The Falconer on the Canterbury Road. He was drinking in the lounge bar when McKee telephoned and he took the call in the public box in the hall.

McKee said guardedly, 'I'd like you to pick up an order for me this afternoon if you would.'

'I'll try, but it will depend on whether or not I have to go out of my way.'

'It'll entail a small detour. The address is Silk's Off Licence, 178 London Road, Bagshot—you're expected.'

Calvert said, 'When do you want to take delivery?'

'Today at Hillglade Farm—any time before seven. Get yourself a map and make sure you don't get lost. I don't want you asking the way to Melton Basset.'

'I'll do my best.'

'You'd better,' said McKee.

Calvert hung up and left the booth. He had learned that it was unwise to argue with McKee, and he lunched quickly before telephoning his customers in Deal and Folkestone to explain why he wouldn't be calling on them that afternoon. By one-thirty he was on the way to Bagshot and making good time in the Cortina estate.

Silk's Off Licence was the end shop in the arcade, and Calvert ran his car into the delivery yard and then knocked on the back door. It was opened by a blonde in her early forties who was wearing a brief mini-skirt and skin-tight black boots which reached up to her plump thighs. Calvert wondered why it was always the women with the fattest legs who still clung to the shortest minis.

He said, 'We haven't met before; I'm Calvert. I think Mr Silk has an order ready for me to collect.' It was no lie; until Sunday he hadn't met Silk.

The woman said, 'I'm Janet Silk, Reg is in the stock-room. You'd better come inside.' She moved ahead, her large buttocks undulating beneath the skirt and the tights made a curious rasping sound as her thighs rubbed together.

She threw open the door to the stock-room and said, 'There's a Mr Calvert here to see you, Reg.' Her voice was harsh and grating and, seeing them together for the first time, Calvert was not surprised that she was the taller of the two. Her manner also suggested that metaphorically she wore the trousers.

Silk pointed to a large cardboard box, and said, 'Can you manage it on your own?' The box was six feet in length, stood three feet high and was about two foot broad.

Calvert said, 'Think I've got arms like an octopus, then? You take one end.' It was not as heavy as he had expected but it was still an awkward load to get through the narrow entrance of the stock room and he skinned his knuckles on the door frame. Calvert wasn't exactly in the best of tempers by the time they had stowed it away in the Cortina Estate and he could have used a cold beer, but despite a broad hint, Silk didn't offer him one. The prospect of a longish drive up to Northamptonshire didn't thrill him either.

Calvert had it easy enough on the M1 as far as Northampton but thereafter he ran into every kind of hazard on the narrow, twisting country roads. It seemed to him that just about every farmer in the county had decided that it was a good time to move livestock, and if it wasn't a herd of cows that barred his way, it was some damned yokel ambling along on a tractor. Despite being forced to a crawl at times, he still made Hillglade Farm well before six.

He swung into the yard and parked the car opposite the rear

porch. An Alsatian, lying in the shade of the stable block, rose up and advanced towards him snarling. Calvert decided it was safer to stay inside the Cortina until someone came to meet him. No one appeared from the stables or the barn to see what the noise was about, but above and behind him, a window opened and a voice called, 'Don't worry about the dog, he wouldn't hurt a fly.' The window closed with a bang, and shortly afterwards McKee appeared on the back porch with Ruth Burroughs, and Calvert judged it was then safe to leave the car.

McKee said, 'Don't tell me you're frightened of that bloody dog?'

Calvert ignored the question. 'I've got your order,' he said, 'where do you want it put?'

'In the cellar. I'll give you a hand with it.'

The cellar was cool and musty but it was getting a little crowded. The wine racks had been shoved together to make space for the bed, but even so, there was very little room to move about in. The boy, of course, wasn't moving anywhere. He was lying spreadeagled on the bed, his legs and wrists chained to the bedposts. As McKee pointed out, they didn't make beds like that any more and they had been lucky to pick it up in a sale. The boy's appearance came as a shock to Calvert. He looked unkempt and his pallor seemed unhealthy. The gag wadded into his mouth was not only crude and effective but also added to his air of misery.

McKee caught him looking at the boy and said, 'Don't worry about him, he'll live. If you've got a knife, we'll see what Silk has sent us.'

Without a word, Calvert took out his clasp-knife, slashed the lid and ripped it open. Reaching inside the box, he brought out a Number 5 Lee Enfield rifle, a Mark II Sten machine carbine, two Colt ·38 automatics and a Springfield ·30 calibre carbine.

McKee smiled at him and said, 'That's right, I'm thinking of starting a war.'

'Jesus.'

'Oh, come on,' said McKee, 'don't look so worried, it was only a joke.'

The guns seemed to have a curious effect on Ruth Burroughs. Her eyes were on McKee, and reading the expression on her face, Calvert thought that if he were Paul Burroughs, he would make a point of keeping a watchful eye on his preserves.

They had reached the point where their lives were now dominated by a few pounds of plastic, copper wire and cheap metal. The telephone was no longer a means of communication but was instead an efficient apparatus for extortion. Wray and Harper joined them shortly before seven, and they sat in anguished silence waiting for its harsh summons. It rang at 7:15 pm and Tarrant answered it.

Drabble said, 'I don't want to speak to you, put Harper on.'

Harper said, 'I'm listening.'

'Good; now perhaps we can get down to business. Did you get the bill of sale?'

'Of course.'

'Now that really sounds too glib. I mean, it isn't every day of the week that you spend half a million, is it?'

'No.'

'Well, all right then, let's be a little more precise. What have you done with the diamonds?'

'I have them in my office safe.'

Drabble said, 'They should be safe enough in there for the time being. Now all you have to do is post the receipted bill to 268 Upper Street, Wealdstone, and make sure it gets there by the second delivery tomorrow.'

'That's impossible, we've missed the last collection.'

'Oh, come on, you can do better than that, Harper. The last collection in your area is seven-thirty and there is a pillar-box a few yards from the house. You've got nearly fifteen minutes to make it. I'll call you tomorrow as soon as I have the bill of sale.'

'What was that address again?'

'You must think I was born yesterday. You already have it on tape.'

Harper said, 'One other point, before we go any further—we want proof that David is still alive.'

Drabble said, 'You know, I expected you to bring that up. Listen to this.'

The tape hissed briefly and then David said, 'We listened to the news on BBC 1 at five-fifty tonight. There was a bank raid in Croydon; five masked men armed with pick helves, a sawn-off shotgun and ammonia dispensers got away with twenty thousand pounds.' The tape ended, the line was disconnected.

Tarrant said, 'Thank Christ, he's still alive.'

'Yes, at least we have that to be thankful for,' said Harper. He avoided Tarrant's eyes and looked up at the ceiling. 'And it will also be interesting to see how Drabble intends to make the collection.'

Wray said, 'I don't believe he'll be that stupid, but all the same, we'll throw a tight surveillance net around the address in the hope of getting a lead.'

They might have been discussing which horse they should back in the two-thirty and he heard Alex draw in her breath sharply and her hand sought his wrist and her nails bit into the flesh.

Tarrant said, 'Let's be clear about one thing, I don't give a damn about catching Drabble, I just want to get my son back.'

'It comes to the same thing, doesn't it?' Harper said mildly. 'After all, if we don't catch him, what guarantee have you that you will ever get your son back alive?'

Wednesday

FOURTH DAY

5

IT WAS JUST LIKE ANY OTHER HIGH STREET IN THE SUBURBS with its Boots, Sainsburys, United Dairies and Co-operative Society. Number 268 Upper Street, which was four doors along from the Midland Bank, belonged to a newsagent who provided an accommodation address. Plain-clothes men were keeping the shop under surveillance from the Linden Café on the opposite side of the street and the adjacent side roads. With the co-operation of the owner, a man had also been placed inside the shop itself. Two Q cars, one facing north, the other south, were in a position to shadow the suspect in case he should use a vehicle. The surveillance team was operating on a special net which had been allocated its own frequency so that, being divorced from normal police radio traffic, control became much tighter and the risk of intercept was minimised.

Wray was sitting in a Ford Escort which was in a parking bay a hundred yards up the road from the shop. The time was eleven-thirty and the second postal delivery was almost due. The street was crowded with shoppers, mostly women.

CID had objected to his presence on the grounds that the investigation of a kidnapping was not his concern, and on the whole, Wray was inclined to agree with them. Relations between CID and the Special Branch had never been exactly cordial and the Tarrant affair had merely exacerbated the situation. The fact that only Wray and a constable from the uniformed branch were allowed to be present when Drabble called and that CID had been shut out for reasons which the Assistant Commissioner had failed to make entirely clear, had already led to a drying up in the exchange of information between the two departments. No one regretted this more than Wray.

Some eight months previously, Special Branch had received a tip that Penfold was The Contractor. The tip had come from a low grade source and had been provisionally graded F6—*informant unproven and possibly unreliable, information unconfirmed and probably untrue.* Nevertheless, for the next three months, Wray had kept the Swiftsure Detective Agency under observation before he had reluctantly come to the conclusion that the provisional assessment had been right. But now he was not quite so sure; for quite illogical reasons, he had a hunch that there was a connection between Penfold and the two, as yet, unidentified men who had been murdered on the A170. It was no use crying over spilt milk, but Wray wished that he was still being kept informed of the progress of the investigation into both killings.

Wray opened the glove pocket, took out his pipe and carefully filled it from the tin of Three Nuns tobacco. He struck a match and held it over the bowl; spittle bubbled in the pipe stem and then a plume of blue-grey smoke rose up and hung in a thin veil below the curved roof. He wound the window down on his side and allowed it to escape. Smoking, he maintained defensively, always helped him to think more clearly.

He was slowly coming round to the view that Chesterman was probably wasting his time prying into Tarrant's personal affairs. There might have been some point in going on with it if they had been able to show that Drabble's letter had been typed on Tarrant's portable, but such was not the case. And now all they had to work on was the fact that Tarrant had been, and possibly still was, on intimate terms with a woman called Barbara whom he saw regularly for lunch. Colonel Mulholland had told Harper that, as far as he knew, Tarrant's lunch break rarely extended beyond an hour and a half, and in view of this time factor, it seemed reasonable to assume that they met locally and that the woman was also employed in the Ministry of Defence. Chesterman was faced with the task of checking out an army of civil servants to find one who answered to the name of Barbara and who had red hair.

The silent radio net came to life. A voice said, 'Zero, this is watchdog one—the post has just been delivered to this location but no letter addressed to the suspect has been received. Please advise, over.'

Control, like Wray, was at a loss to know what to advise. It seemed strange that the letter had failed to get there on time unless it had been wrongly sorted, but since it had been clearly addressed, this didn't seem a likely explanation.

Watchdog One came up on the air again. He said, 'I've just been checking with the proprietor—he tells me he's never heard of Drabble.'

Wray emptied his pipe into the ashtray, started the car and backed out of the parking bay. He thought it was about time he had a chat with the local postmaster.

Their short talk was to prove interesting. Drabble, sure of how the police would react, had filled in a change of address form so that, although Harper had sent the bill of sale to 268 Upper Street in accordance with his instructions, the sorters at the local post office had automatically redirected it to the new forwarding address at 57 Maple Drive.

57 Maple Drive was a business premises belonging to a Mr Roscoe of Roscoe Motors. One look at the place was enough to convince Wray that it was bent. A large detached house had once stood on the site of number 57 but in October 1940, a lone Heinkel 111 which had drifted away from the main bomber stream, decided to go for the railway line and released a stick of six 250 kg bombs. Three fell on the embankment, three didn't, and one of those which missed the target neatly levelled the house. Two months later a bulldozer arrived, and after it had

filled in the crater, a long pre-fab hut was erected, and the bomb site became an Emergency Ambulance Station. After the war, the site had had a checkered history, becoming a junk yard, a builder's yard and finally, Roscoe Motors.

Roscoe specialised in rebuilding insurance write-offs. From two wrecks costing about fifty each, he would produce one road-worthy car which, after respraying, was sold at an average profit of three hundred per cent. He was the sort of man who had several bank accounts and excited the curiosity of the Inland Revenue. By the time Roscoe acquired the site, the original hut had already suffered a number of structural alterations, and the changes he made only added to the general air of delapidation. His office, separated from the workshop by a hardboard parti-tion, was chaotic. Letters, bills, invoices and consignment vouchers littered the top of the worm-ridden desk.

Roscoe was short, dark, stockily built, thirty and very fly. He had so far managed to stay on the right side of the local law, who suspected that he was about as straight as a corkscrew.

Wray showed him his ID Card and said, 'I have reason to believe that a letter addressed to a Mr Drabble was delivered here this morning.'

Roscoe smiled warmly. 'That's right,' he said cheerfully, 'he collected it about half an hour ago. He arrived minutes after the postman. I thought it funny at the time.'

'Why?'

'It wasn't the usual arrangement; normally I opened his mail for him.'

Wray said, 'I don't believe it.'

'Straight up,' said Roscoe. 'It was part of the arrangement, squire, he didn't want any letters reaching him from a certain party—he'd put some bird up the stick and didn't want a main-tenance order slapped on him. Anyway, he would call me each morning, ask if there was anything for him, and if there was, I had to read it out to him over the phone.'

Wray said, 'Apart from this morning's letter, how many others did you receive and read?'

'Only one, from a bird called Doreen something or other.'

'Have you still got it?'

'It's here somewhere on the desk.' He rummaged through a pile of invoices and came up with an envelope. 'Here,' he said, 'read it for yourself if you don't believe me.'

The envelope was postmarked Wembley and the letter had been written on a single sheet of cheap, lined paper. The long-hand was backward sloping and untidy and the biro had left smudges all over the text. There was no address at the top and the letter read:

Dear Ted,

I expect your surprised to get this but your landlady told me you was working for Roscoe Motors now, so I hope this letter finds you. I don't know what you think your playing at Ted, but like I told you I'm pregnent and I want to know what you'll do about it. I shall have to stop work in a couple of months and then there will be no more money coming in and my mum and dad cant suport me and the baby. You know he only works part time now on account of his bad heart. Its no good saying its not yours because it is and I want you to do something quick.

Love,
Doreen

Spelling was not her strong point and the grammar would have pained Fowler.

Wray tucked the letter back into the envelope. 'Are you try-ing to tell me that you went to all this trouble for a complete stranger?'

'It wasn't exactly a favour,' said Roscoe, 'he tipped me a fiver to do it for a month, and he wasn't exactly a stranger either—he used to work for me.'

'For how long?'

'About a fortnight—casual labour, see. Look, I've got to be honest with you, I employ a lot of moonlighters, blokes who take a second job at nights, and they want paying in cash, see, because that way they don't pay any tax, and I don't mind because I don't have to bother with insurance stamps and the like. So this Drabble says he's a panel-beater and I take him on, and I was sorry to lose him when he had to leave.'

'Describe him,' Wray said impatiently.

'Well, he was a short, thickset man—had ginger hair, a bit ugly like what with that wart on his eyelid. I'd say he was over forty.'

'And he put this Doreen in the club?'

Roscoe grinned. 'What's age got to do with being randy?' he said.

'All right,' said Wray, 'put your jacket on and let's go.'

'Where to?'

'I'm taking you round to the local nick.'

'Fucking hell,' said Roscoe, 'that's what comes of doing a favour. Will I be there for long?'

'About thirty years if I have anything to do with it,' said Wray.

Tarrant was beginning to live a lie, and the cause of it was the small package nestling in his jacket pocket. It had arrived by second post addressed to him in an unfamiliar hand and Tarrant had thought that strange since very few people were aware that he was staying with Alex. Some instinct had cautioned him to open it in complete privacy, and like a guilty schoolboy smoking his first cigarette, the lavatory had seemed the safest place.

The small, brown paper parcel had contained a compact C-30 cassette and a brief note which read, 'You want to be alone in a quiet place where no one can disturb you when you play this back.' The note was signed by Drabble and the postmark was illegible.

He had thought of his Japanese Hit Parade tape recorder in the flat off Thessaly Road, and somehow he had managed to pick his way through lunch when all the time he had longed to get away and play the tape, and he had racked his brains for an excuse to leave Alex, and finally he had told her that he needed to pick up some clean shirts and underwear, and he had known from the expression in her eyes that she had been unconvinced.

Tarrant drove badly through the early afternoon traffic, and he was a long way from being alert, and because his mind was on the tape, he failed to notice that he was being followed. Yesterday, Special Branch had used a Vauxhall Viva, today it was a Morris 1100.

Tarrant parked the Zephyr in the basement garage, took the lift up to the eighth floor and entered his flat. He made straight for the tape recorder, placed it on top of the writing desk, inserted the cassette and then punched the button marked play back.

Drabble said, 'You don't want the volume up until I tell you. I'll give you just ten seconds to tone it down.'

It was the longest ten seconds of Tarrant's life. The scream came high and ended in a fit of sobbing, and then a terrified boy said, 'Please, please, Mr Drabble, please don't do that again.' The tape hissed briefly and then the scream came again, and this time it was even worse.

In Aden he had seen a petrol tanker go up with the driver still trapped inside the cab and the man had screamed like a demented animal as the flames consumed him, but bad as that moment had been, it was now insignificant when measured against David's cry of agony. The sweat ran down Tarrant's face and the bile rose in his throat; it was as if someone had kicked him in the testicles. He failed to hear Drabble's command to turn up the volume and, missing the first part of the message, he was forced to rewind and start again.

Drabble said, 'David's fingernails hadn't been cut for a week or two, so it was really quite easy to break the heads off two safety matches and wedge them under the nails against the quick. We lit them with another match, Tarrant, and I regret to say that his nails might have to come off. Of course, whether he keeps the other six and his thumbnails is entirely up to you.' Drabble cleared his throat. 'You're going to Paris tomorrow,' he said. 'Harper won't like it, but after I've spoken to him, he won't raise any objection, even though you will be carrying half a million pounds worth of diamonds on your person. He'll insist on providing an escort, but that isn't going to worry you, Tarrant, because you will give them the slip on the Métro at Chaussée d'Antin. You'll make your way to Rolands—it's a bar in the Rue de Tanger just off the Place Stalingrad. Don't be in a hurry to get there, take one hour to cover your tracks from the time you give them the slip on the Métro.' There was a very brief pause and then Drabble said, 'I don't have to tell you what will happen to your son if you foul this up. I want you to get the details clear in your mind and then you will wipe this tape clean.'

He sat there staring at the now silent tape recorder, unable to move, unable to think clearly, unable to feel anything except a numbness such as is induced by a shot of cocaine into a nerve end. And then presently, he lit a cigarette and played the recording again and yet again until he knew exactly what was expected of him, and then, being sure, he wiped the tape clean and put the recorder away.

Tarrant got up and walked into the bedroom and stripped off, hurling his clothes on to the floor. He went through the chest of drawers looking for a clean change of socks and underwear and a sharp point pricked his thumb, and there they were —four medals on a bar.

And now he saw again that day in Queen Arwa Road when the blazing sun had turned the township into a furnace, and he was pinned down behind the riddled Land-Rover with his driver and wireless operator lying dead in the deserted street. And he couldn't radio for help because the set was smashed, and the back-up Land-Rover had been hit by an RPG 7, and the hidden snipers were going to stay and fight this one out because they knew that Tarrant was alone. And he had been forced to crawl out into the open to recover the phosphorous grenade from the dead operator because he needed something to blind the snipers if he was going to get out of the ambush alive, and he had been lucky, for in their excitement, the guerrillas had fired wildly. And then he had thrown the grenade at the houses facing him, and under cover of the thick white smoke, he had dashed across the street, ripped open the shutters on the ground-floor window and gone in head first. And he knew that they would try to get out on to the flat roof, and when he reached the landing the first man had almost disappeared through the trap-door, and the second man, whose back had been used as a springboard was still bent double when Tarrant thrust the rifle into his open mouth and squeezed the trigger. Above him, two spindly legs thrashed the air in wild panic as the first man attempted to lever himself up, and Tarrant had shot him without compunction, and then he had killed the frightened boy who had run out of the room behind him and who, at the last minute, had tried in vain to surrender.

He remembered that boy well, a thin boy who seemed almost emaciated, and who had found it difficult to hold the AK 47 Kalashnikov automatic rifle in his small hands, and looking back now over the years, Tarrant realised that he must have been close to David's age. He saw the tired reflection of his face in the mirror. 'You and me, Drabble,' he said aloud, 'what's the difference between us?'

Fear was being replaced by a consuming hatred and a deep rooted conviction that somehow, somewhere, he would extract payment in full from Drabble, but until that opportunity arose, Tarrant would act like a pliant tree and bend with the wind. He would mask his feelings as he had been trained to do; he would, if necessary, betray everything he represented to preserve David's life until he was out of harm's way, and then, by Christ, even if it took him twenty years, he would track down and kill Drabble.

He turned away angrily and started to lay out an additional change of clothing on the bed because he didn't want Alex to know that he had been lying. The telephone summoned him in the middle of packing and he went into the other room to answer its strident call.

It was Alex, and her voice was stretched tight like a piano wire. She said, 'Drabble has been in touch again and I don't know how to get hold of your Mr Harper.' Her voice rose and the words came separately as if each required a special effort of will-power to get them out. 'YOU HAD BETTER DO SOMETHING ABOUT IT, JOHN, BECAUSE HE IS TORTURING DAVID. YOU HEAR ME? HE'S TORTURING OUR SON.'

It took him all of fifteen minutes to calm Alex down and then he phoned Harper.

6

HARPER WAS WAITING FOR HIM ON THE PAVEMENT AS Tarrant pulled up outside the flat and got out of the Zephyr.

He eyed the grip in Tarrant's hand and said, 'You chose an odd time to leave your wife on her own.'

'I didn't know Drabble was going to call her.'

'No,' Harper said coldly, 'no, I don't suppose you did, and of course you also wouldn't know that Drabble has collected the bill of sale.'

'How?'

'Because of a lack of foresight on our part.' Harper walked up the short flight of steps and rang the bell. 'He's made fools of us, Tarrant. He's too clever for words, isn't he? Keeps one jump ahead all the time.'

'He's going to make a mistake sooner or later.'

'You think so?'

'I know so.'

'I wish I shared your confidence,' Harper said acidly.

Alex opened the door and stood to one side to let them enter. Her eyes told him that she had been crying and when she puffed on the cigarette, Tarrant noticed that her hand was shaking. He remembered that she had given up smoking soon after they had married and, except for a brief period when Sarah had been killed, she had never reverted to the habit. She rarely drank either, but the whisky was strong on her breath. Tarrant put out a hand in sympathy but she appeared to shrink away, and he allowed his arm to drop.

Harper said, 'Your husband tells me that Drabble has been in touch with you, Mrs Tarrant?'

She swallowed hard. 'It's all there on the tape,' she said. 'I don't think I could listen to it again.'

'I expect it must have been very harrowing for you.' Harper meant to be considerate but the words sounded trite and Alex ignored him.

Looking at Tarrant, she said, 'If you want me, I'll be in my room.' She left them outside the lounge with a curt nod of dismissal, and Tarrant could see that Harper felt awkward, but he made no attempt to excuse Alex's behaviour. He figured that if Harper couldn't see for himself that she was overwrought, he would have to be peculiarly insensitive. And in a way he was, for Harper was in no mood to prevaricate. As soon as they entered the lounge, he told the duty policeman to play back the latest tape.

It began with Alex. She said, '9984.'

The bleeps started and then ceased abruptly as the coins were fed into the box.

'Mrs Tarrant?'

'Yes, who's speaking?'

'Drabble—you should know me by now. Is your husband in?'

'No, he's out, he'll be away for about an hour.'

'Well, I suppose if this conversation is being taped, it hardly matters who I speak to, does it?'

'If you say so,' she said in a dull voice.

There was a pause lasting a few seconds during which time Drabble apparently debated whether or not to ring off. In the event, he didn't.

'I'll take delivery of the diamonds tomorrow at noon and in Paris. It has to be Paris, and your husband will be the courier because we know him by sight and no one else will do. He will go to the Cercle National des Armées in the Place Saint-Augustin, where he will wait until we contact him. For obvious reasons, I will now pause for about fifteen minutes and then call you again. Until I do, you must stay away from the telephone, Mrs Tarrant, because I don't want to hear an engaged signal when I come back to you.'

There was a few seconds of silence and then a flat voice said, 'This message was timed at 14:38 and lasted for one minute twenty-eight seconds. Attempts to trace the call ended in failure.'

Harper looked at the duty policeman. 'Did you record those comments?' he said.

The man nodded and placed a finger against his lips.

Alex said, '9984.'

'Just to make it very clear to you, Mrs Tarrant, we expect your husband to arrive at the Paris RV at twelve noon, give or take five minutes either way. Incidentally, we don't want Mr Harper to come up with any bright ideas. This should help to convince him that we mean business . . .'

The scream started high and tailed off into a fit of sobbing, and Tarrant knew that it would rise again as soon as he heard David say, 'Please, please Mr Drabble, please don't do that again.' It was but a small consolation to know that Drabble had made another track of the original recording.

Harper said, 'Kill it, I've heard enough.' He turned and stared at Tarrant. 'I suppose that was your son?' he said slowly.

'Jesus Christ, of course it was.'

'I just wondered.'

'If you don't believe me, ask Alex—you saw the expression on her face when we arrived here.'

'Yes; I also saw the look on your face just a minute ago. You know what surprised me, Tarrant? You showed little sign of emotion.'

'I've been trained to hide my feelings.'

'They seem to know you by sight—any idea why?'

'I expect it's because they've been watching me for bloody weeks.'

Harper said, 'Somehow I thought you would make that point. Now it seems that I really will have to purchase those stones.'

'What?'

'You seem surprised,' Harper said mildly. 'Surely you didn't expect me to lay out half a million pounds when I could persuade the firm to let me have a receipted bill of sale for nothing, did you?'

'So what happens now?'

'I go out and buy the diamonds from Rand and Goodbody while you get in touch with your mother-in-law. You'd better ask her to drop everything and get down here by six o'clock before we collect you.'

'We?'

'Drew, Vincent and myself. We're going to find out how well you can shoot. With half a million pounds at stake, I do not intend to take any chances.'

'I won't let you down.'

'What a curious thing to say, Tarrant. Perhaps, like me, you don't believe that this is just a simple case of kidnapping?'

'I don't know what you believe.'

'Don't you? It's really very simple. Someone is being bought out, and I want to know who it is.' He turned away from Tarrant. 'Don't bother to come to the door,' he said, 'I can see myself out.'

Tarrant followed him out into the hall and cut short any protest from Harper before it could begin. 'Don't fret,' he said, 'I'm just going to see how Alex is.'

He found her, not in her own bedroom but in David's. She was sitting on the floor, her back resting against the bed, and there was an infinitely sad expression on her face.

She looked up as he entered the room and said, 'I came in here to be near him.'

Tarrant sank down on the bed. No matter where he looked, the room bore the stamp of David. Airfix models of a Daring

Class destroyer, a Leander Class frigate and a World War I American four-stack D.M.S. were arranged in line ahead across the front of his desk. *The Complete Sherlock Holmes Short Stories* rubbed shoulders with *Haka! The All Blacks Story, The Second Saint Omnibus* and *Fighting Men and their Uniforms* between book-ends perched on the wide window ledge. Suspended at varying heights from the ceiling were an ME 262, a Lockheed Starfighter and a Hawker Harrier, and pinned to the wardrobe door, was the Esso 1970 World Cup coin collection.

'Are you going to Paris?' she said.

'Yes.'

'With the diamonds?'

'Yes.'

'Somehow I expected Mr Harper to be difficult.'

'He wants to get David back alive as much as you and I do.'

'Are you sure of that?' she said suspiciously.

Tarrant stared at her. 'Listen,' he said tightly, 'Drabble will get everything he's asked for. What more do you want?'

'The truth from you.'

'Christ, we really have reached the end of the road, you and I, haven't we?'

'I think we reached it the day Sarah was killed.'

'You blame me for that, don't you?'

Alex didn't answer him; she looked down and fiddled with the hem of her skirt.

'Sarah was killed in a road accident. It wasn't your fault, it wasn't mine, and it certainly wasn't the truck driver's. It happened because she ran across the road without looking. If I had been in England, if we had been living together, it still wouldn't have made the slightest scrap of difference.'

Alex said, and her voice was listless, 'I was going to meet her, I usually did you know, but it was my birthday and you telephoned me from Aden just as I was about to leave, and but for that, I would have been there on time.'

'Oh, love,' he said gently, 'you forget there was a Lollipop

Lady on duty to see the kids across the road but Sarah ignored her.'

'You always were good at seeing things in a rational light,' she said listlessly. 'I never could. I don't know what I'll do if anything should happen to David.'

'He'll come home safe,' said Tarrant, 'you have my word for it.'

She turned and rested her head in his lap and her soft, chestnut hair brushed against his hands. 'Will you be in danger?' she said.

'Where? In Paris?'

'Yes.'

'No, I don't think so—Harper is bound to send someone to look after me. He thinks it would be a wise move if your mother came down this evening and stayed with you.'

'And you, what do you think?'

'I think it would be for the best while I am away.'

'Poor John,' she said softly, 'you don't like her much, do you?'

'It's a mutual feeling. Will you phone her, or shall I?'

'I will.'

'Well, that's settled then.' He leaned down and kissed her on the lips. It was a long time since he had done that without Alex drawing her head away from him.

'I want David back more than anything else in the world,' she whispered. 'You hear me?'

'I hear you,' he said.

They always went for a walk on Wednesday afternoons when the boy came home from school providing the weather was fine, and the old man and his grandson followed a set route which never varied. Walking east from Coxwold in the direction of Ampleforth, they stuck to the country road until they came to the narrow lane which led up to the gravel pit. Up to that point the dog was always kept on the lead, but once they turned into the lane, the mongrel bitch was allowed to run free. It was also their habit to rest at the top of the lane while the dog wandered off to explore the gravel pit and the surrounding area.

It was possible to descend to the level of the water on the south side of the pit by means of a track which, in the past, had been used by the mechanical grabs to reach the shelf from where they could operate. The dog, more often than not, would find its way down to the shelf where it would wait until the boy, from above, threw a stick into the water which it would then retrieve. On that particular Wednesday afternoon, there was only one minor change in this long-established ritual. The dog, instead of retrieving the stick, returned with a sodden piece of clothing hanging from its jaws.

It was the boy who discovered that it was a brand-new combat jacket, but its presence in the gravel pit aroused the curiosity of the old man whose common sense and twenty-five years experience in the police force before he retired, convinced him that it hadn't got there by accident. In looking for an explanation, he came across a faint set of tyre marks which, in leaving the track, made straight for the gravel pit and ended abruptly at the edge of a sheer drop. Following this discovery, they returned to the village where the old man reported the matter to the local police constable who, after some discussion, decided to refer it to the Inspector at Thirsk.

After due deliberation, the police at Thirsk telephoned 83 Corps Engineer Regiment at Ripon and asked them if they could provide two frogmen to search the gravel pit near Coxwold. At 5:40 pm the Sapper party arrived and commenced diving. They located the overturned Land-Rover and reported that, as far as they could see, no one was trapped inside it. The vehicle, they said, belonged to the 10th Parachute Battalion, Territorial Army Volunteer Reserve and its registration number was 66 WD 54.

A check subsequently showed that none of the vehicles on charge to the 10th Parachute Battalion was missing. The computer at Headquarters Vehicle Organisation revealed that there was no army vehicle with that registration number.

In Harper's world, twenty thousand pounds was enough money to keep an underground press running for a year in Czechoslovakia. For one hundred thousand pounds he knew where he could purchase twenty reconditioned Shermans armed with seventeen-pounder guns, and the same source would, for a further ten thousand, provide Harper with sufficient Armour-Piercing Discarding Sabot ammunition to give each tank fifty rounds. Apart from hardware, Harper also bought and sold men on occasions, but he had yet to meet one who was worth half a million.

Those who passed information were either bought, suborned or did it for free. The really big fish like Oleg Penkovsky or Kim Philby were probably worth five hundred thousand, but they didn't ask for payment; their kind were motivated by political convictions. Those who were suborned because they were perverted or had something to hide, didn't have to be paid either, but it was politic to slip them a little gift now and then to keep them happy. Those who sold information were petty, greedy and small people who had no true idea of their value, and they could be had for a few hundred pounds. But this man, who demanded half a million pounds in uncut diamonds, was really someone rather special. He knew precisely how much he was worth and evidently there were people around who were prepared to see that he got it.

Harper studied the list of names he had scribbled down on the sheet of foolscap. They embraced every single member of the General Purpose Intelligence Committee, and in his view, there was not one man on the list who was worth more than fifty thousand. Certainly, no single naval, army or air force Intelligence officer would fetch that amount of money on the transfer market unless, for some reason, he had access to Cabinet Papers, but someone in MI5 or the Secret Intelligence Service or MI6 might just command such a fee, and the Russians or the Chinese or even the CIA would be interested. He thought it would be just like the CIA to buy someone with money put up by a British Intelligence Agency; it was the sort of move which would appeal to their sense of humour.

He had already spoken to the spooks in MI5 who were concerned with counter intelligence, but they were either hugging it close to their chests or else they really were unable to give him a lead. MI6 would never tell him anything because they had become very sensitive after Blake had shopped their people in Eastern Europe, but Edward Julyan might be able to help. As one of the principal controllers in the SIS, Julyan had a wide range of contacts, and they had known one another for years.

Harper called him on the office scrambler. He said, 'I have a problem, Edward, and I wondered if you could help me solve it?'

'You know me, Cedric,' said Julyan, 'if it is within my power to help, I will.' Julyan was not only a popular and handsome man, he also possessed natural charm.

'Someone on the General Purpose Intelligence Committee is evidently worth half a million pounds to the opposition. I wondered if you had any idea who he might be?'

There was a longish pause and then Julyan said smoothly, 'I can't think of anyone, apart from you and I, Cedric, and of course Poppleton of MI5. Does he have to be a member of the committee? We'd certainly pay that amount to get our hands on—say Marshal Zhukov for example. I imagine they would give a like sum for one of our Cabinet Ministers or any Permanent Under-Secretary come to that. Who's putting up the money?'

'I am,' Harper said grimly. 'I'm being blackmailed into it.'

'Good God.'

'Payment is to be made in uncut diamonds.'

'Clever.'

'Is it?'

'Oh yes, if your man knows a good cutter, the stones could well appreciate in value.'

'Are you free this evening?'

'Well . . .'

'I thought you might like to have dinner with Muriel and me?

It's been quite some time since we had the pleasure of seeing Melissa.'

'I'd love to come, Cedric, but I'm afraid Melissa won't be able to make it. She's holidaying in St Malo—I sent her away with the children for a week—she's been a little run down of late and I thought she needed a break.'

'You'd be very welcome to come on your own.'

'Well, thank you, I'd like to very much. About what time?'

'Let's say eight-thirty,' said Harper, 'I still have one or two things to attend to.'

7

As far as Jarman was concerned, Paris was a city in a class by itself; Berlin lived on a knife edge of intrigue, London was a vast seething dormitory and Tokyo was dying from carbon monoxide fumes, but Paris was a beautiful monument. Winter, spring, summer and autumn he had been a citizen of Paris for the last ten years, and he never tired of it. On those occasions when business took him away, he always returned to the capital fresh and eager, like a man with a new mistress.

Jarman had an apartment in the Avenue de la Division Leclerc in the sixteenth arrondissement, which overlooked the Bois de Boulogne, and an office in the Rue Vingt-Neuf Juillet, from which address he ran a travel agency. The office was not large, but it was in a fashionable area, and it offered a splendid view of the Tuileries Gardens beyond the Rue de Rivoli. The business was not large either, but it was prosperous and it was still growing. People who rented a villa or a flat through Jarman were never disappointed because they could be sure that he personally had vetted them.

Only that morning, Jarman had received a postcard from St Malo from a satisfied client. On the reverse side of the picture of St Vincent's gateway, she had written:

'Arrived here on Monday evening and so far the weather has been marvellous. Having a wonderfully lazy time on the beach. So glad you were able to let us have the apartment at 63 Rue de Rampart.'

The card was written in English and signed 'M'.

Jarman leaned back in the chair and folded his arms behind his head. Through the frosted glass window in the door, he could see the shadowy form of Madame Laurent. Madame Laurent was a widow, a dumpy sallow woman who was efficient, loyal, hard-working and best of all—unimaginative. And being unimaginative, she was not in the least bit curious. A younger woman might have wanted to know something of his private life.

At thirty-two, Jarman was still a bachelor and he intended to remain so. Although he despised women, there was a girl-friend in the background, but theirs was a casual relationship. She lived outside Paris in St Germain, and often they didn't see each other for weeks on end, and when they did meet it was merely to sublimate a desire for sex. It was an arrangement which suited both parties.

He heard Madame Laurent close the drawers in the steel filing cabinet and Jarman immediately adopted a more business-like attitude, so that when she came in to say goodnight, he was carefully drafting a letter. Although Jarman frequently stayed behind when she left to go home, Madame Laurent never failed to remind him to lock up. It was one of her few annoying habits. As soon as he heard the door close behind her, Jarman abandoned all pretence of work.

For the greater part of his life, Jarman had been acting out a charade. As far as the concierge of his apartment building knew, he was Marcel Vergat and he had an identity card and a French passport to prove it. He was an Algerian colonist who had returned to Metropolitan France in June 1959, a year after de Gaulle had come to power, and the French police had long been satisfied that he had never been connected with the OAS. He had, in fact, done his national service with the Chasseurs Alpins, and for a short time he had been stationed in Baden Baden. He had moved to Paris when he was demobilised from the army and had immediately gone into business on the strength of a small legacy left to him by an uncle. The real Marcel Vergat had, however, been murdered in Oran by the FLN in the autumn of 1957 and his body had never been found.

The sun, now streaming in through the side window, caught Jarman in profile and emphasised his sharp angular features, and the shaft of light playing across his face made him squint and he was obliged to get up and close the venetian blinds. The drumming sound of the evening rush-hour traffic moving along the Rue de Rivoli reached his ears.

His eyes strayed to the painting of the Place du Tertre which concealed the small wall safe, and for a moment he hesitated before deciding that he might be pressed for time in the morning. He removed the picture, worked the combination and reaching inside the open safe, took out a wad of one hundred franc notes and an American passport which he stuffed into the breast pocket of his jacket. He then closed the safe, spun the combination dial and carefully replaced the picture. The phone trilled exactly on time, and answering it, he said, 'Trinité 98.66.370.'

'Marcel Vergat?'

'Yes.'

'This is Andrew McKee. I wondered if you had had any luck in finding a flat for me?'

Jarman said, 'As a matter of fact, Mr McKee, only this afternoon I managed to find an apartment in the Boulevard de Grenelle which I think might suit you. Unfortunately, the concierge is a little deaf and near-sighted, but I don't think that need concern you.'

McKee said, 'I'm very grateful.'

'You're welcome. When can we expect you?'

'An associate of mine is paying a flying visit to Paris tomorrow and I would like him to view the place before I sign the lease.'

'I understand. When might we see this friend of yours?'

'About twelve noon, I should think,' said McKee.

Jarman replaced the phone, unlocked the drawer in his desk and took out the photograph. He sat there for the better part of an hour studying every feature of the face—the deep lines either side of the mouth and the finer crease marks under the wide-set pale grey eyes, the almost square jaw and the short blond hair—before refreshing his memory of the physical dimensions of height—six feet one inch—and weight—one hundred and seventy five pounds—listed on the reverse side, and not until then was he satisfied that he could recognise Tarrant anywhere. Special Branch were not the only people who could open a locked door with a piece of mica.

Chesterman had thought it was going to be a simple job, but now he had to admit that Wray had been right all along. He had no idea of the immense size of the Ministry of Defence until he started to check through the records of the civilian employees, nor had he appreciated that this vast organisation was spread right across the face of London. Even when he had eliminated the branches in Stanmore and Chessington on the grounds that, since they were in the outer suburbs, Tarrant would have been unable to meet her for lunch, Chesterman was still left with the Admiralty Building, the main War Office Building, the Air Ministry, Horse Guards Parade, Lansdowne House, Old Scotland Yard, Northumberland House and the establishment in Oxford Street.

It was not enough to scan the personnel currently employed in these branches, he also had to take into account the possibility that the woman might have been transferred to the Provinces within the last five months. He was looking for a woman who was in her thirties, who answered to the name of Barbara and who had red or auburn hair. This woman might be married, single, divorced or widowed, and there was no guarantee that Barbara was her first name; it could be just one of a number of Christian names or even an adopted name. Chesterman's own wife, for example, had been christened Ada Jane but to her friends she was Jackie.

At the end of a long day, and with the help of the Defence Ministry's Security Branch, he had narrowed the choice down to half a dozen women, one of whom had been transferred to Bath early in March. Since the security people were unwilling to release these six duplicate identity cards, Chesterman had to ask permission to photograph them. Unfortunately, by the time the initial check had been completed the only person who was able to authorise such a request had already gone home, and Chesterman reluctantly decided that it would have to wait until Thursday morning.

The indoor range at Braintree Hill in Essex used to be the recreation hall and cinema for the inmates of the World War II POW Camp. The original chain-link fence and watch-towers around the perimeter were reminders of the past and some of the wooden huts were still standing with their windows intact; the camp was too remote and too well patrolled by guard dogs to attract vandals. Harper, who cherished a reputation for being droll, referred to it as his place in the country.

They had left Chiswick before Alex's mother had arrived and the journey had taken them less than forty minutes because Drew was driving, and Drew and the Capri 2000 were sympatico. He had carved through the traffic using the short, stubby gear lever as if it were a natural extension of his left arm, and there was no doubt that he had got the best out of the car. Where there was a thirty-mile-an-hour limit, he was rarely doing less than fifty, where the roads were derestricted the needle of the speedometer flirted with the hundred mark.

Drew was twenty-six and very sure of himself. He was every playwright's idea of what an aggressive middle-class young man should look like; Vincent, with his thick black hair, burly frame and sideburns would have been type-cast as a street trader. In fact Drew had been born in West Ham and had left school at fifteen, while Vincent, who was twelve years older, had been educated at Rugby. They were as different as chalk and cheese, but working together, they made a formidable team. Of the two, Tarrant would have preferred it if Vincent had been detailed off to take him through the firing practice but instead he was landed with Drew.

Drew said, 'I don't know whether you have used this type of range before but I will explain how it works anyway.' He pointed towards the stage. 'Up there, instead of a fixed cinema screen, we have a continuously moving belt of white linen against which Vincent will project the film strip. When you shoot at the target, the sound waves will freeze the picture and then we will be able to see whether you've hit anything or not.'

'It's similar to one of our training theatres,' said Tarrant.

'Oh really?' Drew's tone was a masterpiece of studied insolence. 'Well, I don't know how you people in the army shoot, but we don't hold the pistol in an outstretched arm like some eighteenth-century duellist. If the target is five to ten yards away, we hold the pistol two-handed at chest level and keep both eyes open. At a greater range, we bring the weapon up to near eye level and take a more deliberate aim.'

Tarrant said, 'Are you sure there isn't anything else I should know?'

Drew handed him a pair of ear defenders. 'You'll need these,' he said. 'We can't have you claiming a disability pension because your eardrums have been perforated.' He took a 9-mm Walther P38 out of his shoulder holster, removed the magazine from the butt, and cleared the breech before handing it over to Tarrant. 'You'll have to use my gun,' he said, 'and we'll start at the ten-yard point.'

'How many rounds have I got?'

'Six,' said Drew. 'Let's see if you can hit anything with them.'

The lights were dimmed and Tarrant found himself looking down a narrow, poorly lit street of terraced houses. The two men moving towards him on either side of the road were no more than a faint blur, but he noticed that when one moved, the other man covered him forward. Tarrant noted the pool of light around each street lamp and waited until the leading man was silhouetted and in range, and then he fired twice, swivelled and fired twice more, and such was the speed of his reaction, that the crack of the first round merged with the last. The still picture showed that the leading man had been hit in the chest by two bullets spaced less than an inch apart, the more distant target had been shot in the right shoulder and head.

The scene changed to a crowded street in broad daylight. The camera zoomed in on a bank twenty-five yards from Tarrant and focused obliquely on a woman who stood frozen in the entrance. Someone pushed her forward and, losing her balance, she fell off the bottom step. For a split second, the head and shoulders of a masked man were in view amongst the eddying crowd on the pavement and Tarrant, taking deliberate aim, fired once, and then noticing the car pulling away from the kerb, fired again into its windscreen.

Drew removed the ear defenders. 'Why didn't you go for the tyres?' he said.

'You know why,' said Tarrant. 'They're too small a target.'

'I think you had a run of luck.'

'You want to try me again?'

'We're going to,' said Drew.

During the next twenty minutes, Tarrant fired a total of sixty rounds. He shot at men sniping from windows, from behind piles of rubble, at men moving across rooftops and at men climbing, jumping, running, crawling and diving, and these celluloid encounters took place at dusk, in the first light of morning, in thick fog, in driving rain and sleet and in the dead of night. When it was finished, he had recorded a total of fifty-two hits.

Upstairs in the projectionist's box, Vincent turned to Harper and said, 'What gave you the idea he couldn't shoot?'

'Did I say he couldn't?'

'Well, why are we here if there wasn't a doubt in your mind?'

'It's advisable to know what you are up against.'

Vincent rubbed his chin thoughtfully. 'Is he with the opposition, then?'

'I don't know, he might be. It depends on events in Paris tomorrow.'

'You mean he could try to slip us?'

'Perhaps.'

'He would find that difficult if he didn't have any French francs.'

Harper said, 'I've thought about that, but if you or Drew pay for everything, they will know he is being watched and they will avoid making contact.'

'So we shadow him at a distance, is that it?'

'We're after the contact man, not Tarrant.' Harper glanced at his wrist-watch. 'Let's call it a day,' he said, 'I'm going to be late for dinner as it is.'

8

MCKEE GOT OFF THE NOTTINGHAM TRAIN AT KETTERING, surrendered his ticket at the barrier and walked out of the station. He had expected to find Burroughs waiting for him but instead, Ruth was there with her Mini. He opened the door, tossed the briefcase and brown paper bag on to the back seat, and got in beside her. He barely had time to adjust the seat belt before she moved off.

McKee said, 'Why didn't Paul come to meet me?'

'Because I chose to pick you up instead.'

'So he's watching the boy?'

'Well, there isn't anyone else, is there?' she said flippantly.

'You know damn well he could be the weak link, and he's squeamish where the boy is concerned. He might do something stupid.'

'The boy,' she said patiently, 'is locked in the cellar and I've got the keys. You may have promoted Paul out of his class, but he won't do anything silly. He is squeamish about violence, but as long as he is not forced to watch it happening he can be quite objective about it.'

'You should know.'

'I should. Did you have a good day in London?'

'You might say it went off without a hitch. Silk didn't have any trouble collecting the receipt from Roscoe.'

'You were lucky, the police could have been watching the place.'

'Silk was watching from a phone-box up the road, and he can smell a policeman a hundred yards off. If he had been in doubt, he wouldn't have gone near the place.'

'And if the Post Office had failed to deliver it on time?'

'We would have called it off, and our friend would have been forced to trust us.'

McKee lapsed into silence and thought about the man, the very special man on whose behalf they were risking everything. Every night between ten and twelve, that very special man would leave his house in Hampstead to walk his dog over the heath before turning in for the night. The dog would pause at the occasional tree because dogs have a habit of doing that, but tonight the dog would be led to a particular tree and there, in that most simple of all dead letter-boxes, the man would find the bill of sale he wanted so much.

Ruth Burroughs said, 'Were they surprised to see you in the office today?'

'No, why should they be surprised? They knew I was calling in this evening.' McKee undid the safety belt, turned about and picked up the brown paper parcel from the back seat. 'I bought this today,' he said, 'a pair of reins for a toddler.'

'How very kinky. Shall I wear them when I prance round your room in a pair of high-heeled boots?'

She saw the anger in his face and said hastily, 'Sorry, it was a very bad joke.'

'You can make all the bad jokes you like when this job is over.'

'I've already said I'm sorry.'

'All right,' McKee snapped, 'let's forget it. Tomorrow, I want you to make fourteen canvas pouches which we can tie on to this set of reins. Don't look so puzzled, they will serve as our exit visa.'

'I don't understand.'

He laid a hand on her thigh and squeezed it gently. 'You will when the time comes.'

'We haven't got much time left, have we?'

'It should be all over by Saturday.'

'That isn't what I meant.' She looked down at the hand which was caressing her thigh. 'And you know it.'

'There isn't much I can do about that,' he said vaguely.

'Every Thursday, except in the winter months and at harvest time,' she said slowly and deliberately, 'Paul finishes work at four o'clock so that he can have a round of golf with his friends. Now, that is a well-established pattern which, even now, I think he ought to stick to, don't you?'

The house in West Byfleet had cost seventeen fifty when it was built in '36, Harper had acquired it for five and a half thousand in 1958, and now it was worth three times that much. Land hadn't been at such a premium in the thirties, and in consequence, the garden was several times larger than its modern counterpart. Except for the rose beds, it was mostly lawn all the way down to the line of silver birch trees which concealed the railway cutting at the bottom. The house was right in the heart of the commuter belt and, if Harper had anything in common with his neighbours, it was that, like them, he normally caught the 8:18 up and the 6:25 down.

Edward Julyan faced Harper across the oval dining-table; an empty chair marked Muriel Harper's place. Above their heads a pall of smoke eddied below the ceiling like cumulus in the sky, but unlike cumulus, it had a distinctly musty smell. The cigars which Harper had brought back from Amsterdam some three summers ago had lost their freshness.

Julyan said, 'Muriel hasn't lost her touch.'

'What?'

'The dinner, it was quite excellent.'

'Oh yes—Muriel will be pleased.'

'You're very preoccupied.'

Harper's smile was thin. 'If you stood to lose half a million pounds in the morning,' he said, 'wouldn't you be preoccupied?'

'I would if the money belonged to me.'

'I'm still responsible for it, and if anything goes wrong, I'm answerable to the Minister. I virtually guaranteed that if we went along with Drabble, we would catch the defector.'

Julyan examined his cigar. 'If there is a defector,' he said. 'After all, it is just possible that you are faced with a criminal conspiracy.'

Harper said, 'Tarrant is the only person I can think of who has the know-how to set it up, and I don't believe any man would deliberately torture his own son.'

Julyan said, 'In my experience, the really big men in espionage are motivated by patriotism—your man is doing it for the money.'

'And therefore he isn't a spy? Is that what you're implying?'

'Who's paying him? Not the Russians—you are, Cedric.'

'Perhaps he remembers that the Germans paid Cicero off in forged five-pound notes,' Harper said drily.

'Do you know, that thought hadn't occurred to me. You might have something.'

'If I have it's precious little.'

'No, really, let's assume you're right, Cedric. Why did they pick on Tarrant out of all the members of the General Purpose Intelligence committee? Was he the only man with a son away at boarding school?'

'I don't know.'

'What is it about Tarrant that makes him so special?' Julyan stubbed out his cigar. 'If I were in your place, I would want to know everything about Tarrant—his friends, his financial status, his movements over the past few months—that sort of thing.' Julyan smiled deprecatingly. 'But I don't have to give you any advice, Cedric, you're an expert.'

'I've never met an expert yet who couldn't benefit from advice some time or another.'

'Is Tarrant a ruthless man?'

'He won a Military Cross in Aden.'

'Well, there you are then.'

'In my experience, Edward,' Harper said mildly, 'people who win medals for bravery are not necessarily ruthless. As a matter of fact, I spoke to Tarrant's former commanding officer on the telephone this morning, and he gave me an interesting slant on Tarrant's character. Amongst the terrorists he killed in an ambush was a boy of about thirteen. This boy was armed with a Kalashnikov and subsequent investigations proved beyond doubt that he had been firing it, but the interesting point is that Tarrant was torn with feelings of guilt. The boy, it appears, came out of a room with the gun in his hands while the shooting was still going on, and at the last minute, he apparently decided to surrender. Tarrant said that he shot him as he dropped the gun.'

Julyan said, 'I don't wish to sound cynical, but in making that limited confession, he pre-empted the subsequent enquiry, and at the same time won a great deal of sympathy for himself.'

Harper helped himself to another glass of brandy and then pushed the decanter across the table towards Julyan. 'I remember an occasion during the war, Edward,' he said, 'when we were clearing this village in Sicily and the point platoon was about fifty yards in front of my company headquarters, when a young German from the Hermann Goering Division suddenly appeared in a side street. I watched, almost stupefied at his apparent audacity as he fired a burst from his Schmeisser into the backs of the leading platoon and knocked over a couple of my men. And then he saw the rest of the company and suddenly he realised that he had chosen the wrong moment and that, far from hitting the tail end, he'd only caught the leading elements. He hadn't a hope in hell of getting away, so he threw his weapon aside, held up his hands and yelled kamerad for all he was worth. I grabbed my sergeant-major's rifle, Edward, and I shot him, because you see, to my way of thinking, you can't shoot a man in the back and then think you can surrender just because the going has got a little rough. The point is that, if he had stood his ground, I would probably have called on him to surrender.'

'How old were you then, Cedric?'

'Almost twenty. We'd taken a lot of casualties and I was the only surviving officer in the company, but that doesn't excuse the fact that I killed that German. However, unlike Tarrant, I didn't lose any sleep over it, and in my view, it doesn't matter whether the enemy is thirteen or thirty, the gun in his hands kills just the same. Tarrant has a conscience and that's why I don't believe he could set this thing up.'

Julyan said, 'You're probably right, Cedric. Anyway, you know him better than I do.' He glanced surreptitiously at his wrist-watch. 'Much as I would like to stay on,' he said, 'I think I must be leaving. The house is in a bit of a mess since Melissa went on holiday with the children.'

'I thought you had a girl living in?'

'The au pair went with Melissa.'

Harper thought that was typical of her. Melissa was young and attractive and good company but she could be extremely self-centred. As long as she was all right, no one else mattered. Almost as an afterthought, Julyan said, 'Of course, we do have a daily, but she can't walk the dog last thing at night and the odds are that he's probably peeing all over the bloody kitchen this very minute.'

The love–hate relationship between CID and Special Branch had taken a turn for the better and Wray had Roscoe to thank for that; not that Roscoe had been able to tell them very much, but in throwing him their way, CID were duly grateful. It was a gesture which had cost Wray nothing but it had paid considerable dividends.

He sat there alone in the pub clutching his third large whisky and soda and the warm feeling inside him wasn't entirely due to the alcohol. Wray had learned much in the mellowness of a partnership renewed. He now knew that the two men who had been murdered on Sunday had been identified as Goring and

Findon, and a whisper was going around that they had been hired by The Contractor. They'd even built up an identikit picture of the man they thought was the last person to see Penfold alive, but as CID were the first to admit, the picture had its limitations—Gina (Secretarial Services) could not be expected to single out one man amongst all her clients with any degree of accuracy.

They expected to do a little better with James Stroud when they were allowed to question him in the morning, because all they'd got so far from the doctors was an idea of the hallucinations induced by LSD. The boy was great on rampant lions and red devils, especially red devils—he kept on about one big red devil in particular.

Wednesday had been a long hard day and Wray wasn't at his best at the end of it, otherwise he might have appreciated the significance of the continual reference to red devils. Any child with an Action Man toy could have told him that it was a nickname bestowed on the Parachute Regiment, but then Wray didn't have any children.

Thursday

FIFTH DAY

9

THE BEA TRIDENT MADE ORLY AIRPORT IN ONE HOUR and, in the absence of turbulence, it was a smooth ride. Even so, Tarrant failed to get any rest despite a lack of sleep the night before, which he had spent in the loneliness of his flat off Thessaly Road. The arrival of his mother-in-law had made it impossible for Tarrant to stay on with Alex because he wanted to avoid the inevitable acrimony which would have distressed her. Neither party set out with the intention of provoking the other, but somehow it happened just the same when mother and son-in-law met face to face.

They went through Customs and Immigration without any trouble, and Tarrant supposed that they had Harper to thank for that because it wasn't every day that three men, each one of whom was carrying a Walther P38 in a shoulder holster, got off the London plane. And most certainly, it was unusual to see a man chained to a briefcase, but as far as the French were concerned, they appeared to accept it as if it was the most natural thing in the world.

They left the airport in separate taxis, Drew and Vincent following Tarrant at a discreet distance. Tarrant sat in the Peugeot nursing the leather briefcase on his lap while he tried to conceal the length of chain which showed beneath his shirt cuff. From time to time, he moved his right hand across the surface of the briefcase to reassure himself that the diamonds were inside. It was unavailing because he had insisted on seeing the diamonds before they were locked away and naturally, that had annoyed Harper. Even now, Tarrant had a nasty feeling that the stones might just be paste. Logic told him that his fears were groundless but an over-active imagination still plagued him.

Two lines of traffic were coming up from the Boulevard Haussmann, but without warning, the taxi shot across in front of the nearside lane and stopped outside the Cercle National Des Armées. Drew and Vincent drove past the Officers' Club and turned into the next side street on the right. Tarrant paid off the taxi and went inside, to be followed some minutes later by Drew and Vincent.

Their intention was to deceive the opposition but it failed to come off because Jarman had a grandstand view, and he had anticipated that they would try to conceal the fact that Tarrant had an escort. On that pleasantly warm morning in May, Jarman was just one of a number of people who had chosen to use the sidewalk tables outside the café, and from where he sat, he had an unimpeded view of the front entrance to the Cercle National Des Armées some fifteen yards away. His interest in the passing crowd appeared to be minimal and he seemed to be engrossed in the early morning edition of Le Figaro, but his sharp eyes missed nothing. Given the fact that he knew what to look for, spotting Vincent and Drew was not very difficult and there was something about them both which was so obviously English. The way they walked and the cut of their clothes betrayed them. He decided he would let them sweat it out for a bit before he telephoned the reception desk.

With its imposing entrance, crystal chandeliers and the sweeping staircase which led to the floors above, the Club had all the grandeur reminiscent of the First Empire, and Tarrant, seated at one of the tables in the foyer, felt insignificant. Drew and Vincent who were seated at another table also looked ill at ease under the gaze of the clerks behind the long reception counter. There was a stillness and solemnity about the hall which encouraged a hushed tone of voice.

Tarrant was no good at the waiting game and his eyes kept straying to the clock on the wall. He was perspiring freely and the roof of his mouth felt dry and tacky. He wondered if Drew and Vincent would draw the obvious conclusion. Giving them the slip was not going to be easy since he was not familiar with the geography of Paris. He had been there only once before, for a long weekend shortly after he and Alex had been married, and he had forgotten much of what he had seen. He recalled place-names with difficulty, and the more he faced up to the problem, the less confident he became. Once he had given Drew and Vincent the slip, he thought it probable that every *gendarme* in Paris would be on the look out for him.

A voice said, 'Commandant Tarrant?'

The surname was mispronounced and he didn't recognise it at first, but when it was repeated, he looked up, and seeing one of the desk clerks gazing speculatively around the foyer, he got up and walked hurriedly towards him.

'I'm Major Tarrant,' he said carefully.

The man smiled and handed him an envelope. 'This message came for you.'

'Did you see the man who delivered it?'

The desk clerk looked puzzled. 'My English, it is not good,' he said slowly.

Tarrant searched his schoolboy French and in a mixture of both languages, repeated the question. It was something of a small miracle that the man understood.

'The message,' he said emphatically, 'was by the telephone and I was reminded how to deliver it.'

'How?'

The man pointed to the switchboard. 'By the telephone, how else, monsieur?'

The message was meant to be short and to the point, but as it was written in French, Tarrant needed help to translate it and that wasted precious minutes. It said roughly: 'My apologies for not being present to meet you. Suggest you come to my flat at 31 Rue Lancen. Take the Métro to the Place République.— Drabble.'

He noticed that Drew was trying to catch his eye and Tarrant guessed that they wanted to see the note. He walked by their table and entered the washroom, knowing that after a short interval, either Drew or Vincent would follow him. He thought it would be Drew but he was wrong about that.

Vincent said, 'May I see the note?'

Tarrant handed it to him. 'Are you planning to alert the French police?' he said.

'No, we don't know who we are looking for. I don't think they will try anything on the Métro but they may be watching us.' Vincent's face was impassive. 'So we'll play it safe. I'll be in the same carriage with you and Drew will be in the one behind. Okay?'

'Yes.'

'All right, let's get started.'

Tarrant had forgotten what it was like inside the Métro. The warm atmosphere was stifling and it felt as if someone was holding a damp towel close to his face. He stood beneath the sign which indicated the point opposite which the first-class carriage would stop, and Vincent, who was almost within touching distance, made a point of studying the Métro map on the wall in the hope that no one would suspect that they were together. Drew was some way down the platform where he would have the pleasure of riding second-class. A train bound for the Pont de Sèvres pulled into the platform on the other side of the station and hissed to a stop; seconds later, the train they had been waiting for appeared in the tunnel and groaned into the station. A woman bustled in front of them, threw the safety lock off and opened the sliding doors. They followed her into the carriage, Tarrant turning left to take a seat not too far away from the doors, and Vincent moving right to the other end of the compartment and choosing a corner seat where he could keep an eye on Tarrant. The doors closed automatically and then the train crawled out of the station.

There was just one stop between Saint Augustin and Chaussée D'Antin, the station name memorised from Drabble's tape and, although his stomach was turning over, Tarrant did his best to look unconcerned. Drabble had picked the wrong time of day because not many people used the Métro during the lunch hour and Tarrant needed a crowd to help him shake off Drew and Vincent. He planned to slip the train just as the doors were closing, but if that move was to come off, someone would have to get into the carriage at Chaussée D'Antin. The doors closed automatically but they had to be opened manually and he couldn't afford to waste time doing that. No one got into his section of the carriage at the intermediate stop, but at least he was able to calculate the interval between the train stopping and starting.

As the train slid into the next station, his silent prayer that luck would be with him was answered. A family of three got into the compartment and moving to their right, they momentarily screened Tarrant from Vincent's gaze. He left his seat like a greyhound springing out of the trap and he just made it before the doors closed behind him. A woman platform attendant shouted something but he ignored her and hurried towards the exit, and as the train slowly overtook him, he caught a glimpse of Vincent mouthing obscenities at him before he finally disappeared from sight into the tunnel. He felt almost buoyant until he discovered that Drew was following him, and then it came home to Tarrant that the woman had not been shouting at him.

The long, straight subway was wide enough for three people to walk abreast of one another without causing an obstruction, and there was nowhere for him to hide. He knew that he would never be able to shake off Drew unless he was in a crowd and so, in desperation, he made his way up to the street above. Galeries Lafayette was facing him across the road and, dodging through the honking traffic, he slipped inside the nearest entrance. Drew, reading the danger signals, began to close the gap between them.

The department store was crowded with tourists and lunchtime shoppers, and Tarrant thought it was just his bloody luck that when he had wanted a crowd, he had ended up with a milling throng which restricted him to a slow crawl and made it possible for Drew to stay close. He tried a figure of eight around the ground floor, rode the escalator up to the cafeteria on the roof, and still unable to shake Drew, back-tracked down the staircase to the toy department and then, taking to the escalator again, went down to street level. Drew stayed with him all the way and was still almost within touching distance when he came out into the side street.

A cab appeared at just the right moment and Tarrant went into it fast and asked for the Hôtel des Invalides because that was the first address which came into his head. Glancing back over his shoulder, he saw that Drew had also found a taxi and he wondered how he was ever going to lose him. The problem was solved for Tarrant; they just made the lights at the junction of the Rue Mogador and the Boulevard Haussman, but Drew didn't.

The taxi-driver would have been at home on the Le Mans circuit; tyres screaming, wheels drumming over the cobbles, he set out to break the speed limit at every opportunity because, for him, time was money. The buildings flashed by in a confusing blur like film going through a high-speed camera. Tarrant caught a glimpse of the Opera House and the Madeleine, and then they were crossing the Seine beyond the Place de la Concorde, and as soon as they entered the Esplanade des Invalides, he knew he had chosen the wrong place, because in that vast open space, he would be conspicuous, and this was hardly the time to see Napoleon's tomb. He leaned forward and, in halting French, told the taxi driver to stop.

Tarrant paid him off and started walking blindly. The sudden bleeping of a police siren in the distance sent a cold shiver down his back, and he scurried across the open space of the esplanade towards the cafés in the Rue Fabert where he could mingle with the crowds. To his sensitive and mistaken ears, the police car seemed to be drawing nearer and, in mounting fear, he stopped at a magazine stall and turned his back on the road. *Paris Match* rubbed shoulders with the underground press, and next to a paperback whose cover showed two women locked in an embrace, he spotted a Falk street plan of Paris. It cost him six francs but it proved to be a life-saver. He walked into the nearest bar, found a table tucked away in one corner of the room and ordered a coffee. Before he could even begin to think of studying the map, he had to remove the chain which linked him to the briefcase.

Harper had reluctantly decided to let Tarrant have the key to the bracelet because they were playing a waiting game, and the idea was not to arrest the contact but to keep him under surveillance, and for this to succeed, they were prepared to see the diamonds handed over. In taking such a calculated risk, Harper had under-estimated the psychological pressures on Tarrant. With David's life at stake, he was to learn that nothing would be too extreme for Tarrant.

Keeping the briefcase out of sight underneath the table, Tarrant felt for the lock, inserted the key, and turning it anti-clockwise, opened the jaws of the bracelet and freed his wrist. Patiently, and with great care, he hid the loose chain under the covering flap and then placed the briefcase between his ankles. Unencumbered, he was then free to study the map; he spent just over a quarter of an hour in the café memorising the route he would take to Rolands Bar and then he set off at a brisk walk towards the nearest Métro.

Drabble had said that he was to lose himself for an hour, and by the time he had rung the changes on the Métro at Concorde, Châtelet and Gare de l'Est, he arrived at the place Stalingrad on schedule. Jarman, who was waiting in his car across the street from Rolands, saw him enter the bar hugging the briefcase under his arm. So far, it had gone better than Jarman had expected, but being essentially a cautious man, he waited to see if Tarrant was being followed. Within the space of five minutes, he was satisfied that Tarrant was alone, and he pulled away from the kerb and headed across town. He wanted to give himself a head start before he spoke to Tarrant on the phone.

Tarrant was on his second beer and halfway through his third cigarette when the waiter sidled up to him and said, in almost perfect English pronunciation, 'Monsieur Tarrant?'

Tarrant looked up sharply.

'You are Monsieur Tarrant?'

'Yes, I am, how do you know me?'

The waiter shrugged his shoulders Gallic fashion. 'You are as Monsieur Drabble described you, he wishes to speak with you on the telephone.'

'Where?'

The waiter pointed to the phone fixed on the wall near the bar. 'Just there, monsieur,' he said.

Tarrant ground out his cigarette, picked up the briefcase and walked across the room and lifted the receiver.

Jarman said, 'This is Drabble. Have you got the merchandise?'

'Yes.'

'All right, now bring it straight round to 179 Boulevard de Grenelle. I shall be waiting for you in my apartment on the second floor. Have you got that?'

'Yes, I understand.'

'Good. I would remind you that your son's life is in danger.'

Tarrant said, 'Why else would I co-operate with you?' The question didn't get through, Jarman had hung up on him.

There seemed to be no end in sight, and if they kept him running all over Paris as they had been doing, the whole bloody set-up would go sour because Tarrant supposed that, by now, Vincent or Drew would have alerted the French police and his description would be broadcast to every patrol car. His feet pounded a savage tattoo on the pavement as yet again he made his way to the Métro.

Jarman knew that he was cutting it fine, and from the windows of the rented apartment on the Boulevard de Grenelle, he kept an anxious watch on the elevated platform of Bir-Hakeim with his binoculars. With growing uneasiness, he saw train after train pull into the station and then depart, and with each arrival, he told himself that he would see Tarrant emerge on the street below and each time he was disappointed. He began to curse his mania for security, convinced now that his obsession for double-checking every move would be his death. At exactly twenty minutes past two, Tarrant appeared in the entrance to the station and Jarman heaved a sigh of relief.

He moved away from the window, slipped off his shoes, and leaving the door on the latch, crept out into the hall. Jarman had chosen this particular apartment house because it had a steep spiral staircase and, at a point midway between the second and third floors, he knew he would be out of sight from the landing below. He waited there in ambush, and presently he heard Tarrant's footsteps on the staircase, and he counted off each pace because he had to strike at precisely the right moment, and if he bungled it there would be no second chance. The buzzer outside his flat sounded twice, and Jarman came down the stairs like a cat, swung the binoculars in an arc and smashed them against Tarrant's skull. The force of the blow hurled Tarrant into the door which swung open and, since there was nothing to support him now, he fell forward on to his face like an axed tree and lay still.

Jarman dragged him into the flat and closed the door. He slipped his feet back into his shoes, paused long enough to check the contents of the briefcase and then left, locking the door after him. He walked down the stairs as if he hadn't a care in the world, smiled at the near-sighted and almost totally deaf concierge, and then stepped out into the street. His Renault 16 was parked just around the corner of the block.

By three o'clock, he was halfway between Versailles and Dreux and he planned to stay on Route Nationale 12 until he reached Fourgères. He was confident that no one would miss him, least of all Madame Laurent, who earlier that morning had instantly accepted his explanation that he would be away from Paris for a few days on business. He kept a sharp eye out for a phone booth and found a convenient one in the village of Le Mêle-s-Sarthe opposite a filling station.

He checked the dialling code for St Malo and then rang through. When the woman answered, he said, 'This is Marcel Vergat; I wish to speak to Madame Julyan.'

His head felt as though someone had cut loose with a pneumatic drill, and a throbbing nerve end behind his left eye transmitted shock waves of pain which exploded inside his skull. He was seeing everything through a hazy curtain as on a foggy winter's day, and he decided that the room was definitely upside down because the furniture was on the ceiling, and the more he considered it, the more Tarrant became convinced that the grubby ceiling badly needed redistempering, but someone would have to remove the cobwebs first because there were bloody hundreds of them right there in front of his nose. When he managed at last to get up on to his hands and knees, his mind at least was better orientated. He grabbed hold of a chair and slowly pulled himself up on to his feet. His fingers, gently exploring the swelling on he back of his head, came away sticky with blood and he moved unsteadily in search of the bathroom. The cold water felt soothing but its effect on his acting head was only temporary.

Tarrant returned to the other room and tried the door which opened out on to the landing. He rattled it, kicked it, pulled it and put his shoulder against it but the damn thing wouldn't budge. He opened his mouth and yelled at the top of his voice but the only positive reaction that this produced was a distinct feeling that the top of his head had just been sliced off with a cheese cutter.

It came into Tarrant's mind that there ought to be a fire escape but although he searched every room in the apartment, he failed to discover one. He did, however, notice that the sitting-room had a small balcony, and opening the French windows, he saw that the occupants of the adjoining flat had obligingly left their windows open. Ten feet and a nasty drop to the street below were all that separated him from the next balcony. A drainpipe neatly bisected the distance and there was a small ledge which spanned the entire gap. It wasn't all that wide and his heels would be hanging over the edge, but he figured that the drainpipe would give him added support and a couple of good strides ought to do it.

He climbed over the wrought-iron balustrade, swung his left foot across the gap, found a toe-hold, and stretching out his left hand, grabbed hold of the drainpipe. Vertigo nailed him there like a starfish and for several minutes he was unable to move, but then, closing his eyes, he swung the other leg across on to the ledge. He should have straddled the drainpipe, but as it was, the whole of his body was to one side of it and the hand holds were all wrong, and he knew that if he didn't move at once, he was going to fall off. Tarrant went round the obstructing drainpipe like a novice, flailed out with a sweating hand, seized the balcony rails and heaved himself across.

Drawn curtains masked the interior of the room, and pushing them out of the way, he stepped into the gloom, and taking two paces forward he bumped into the bed. The woman reared up like a startled horse, grabbed hold of the sheet to cover her nakedness, and for a moment stared pop-eyed at Tarrant, until finding her voice, she released a piercing scream. Each nerve-jangling cry was louder than the one before, and by the third, the man sleeping beside her had surfaced and was scratching the matt of black hair on his chest. By the time he had thought of getting out of bed to deal with the intruder, Tarrant was half-way down the staircase.

A torrent of abuse followed Tarrant out on to the street, and the concierge stepped out of her room to add to it. The noise alone was enough to attract unwelcome attention, and his unsteady gait heightened a suspicion that he was drunk. Pedestrians gave him a wide berth, but a gendarme on duty at the junction of the Rue du Commerce and the Boulevard de Grenelle took one look at him and summoned a patrol car.

They took him to the Préfecture de Police opposite Notre

Dame and there they held him until Drew and Vincent arrived. Neither man seemed overjoyed to see him but then that was understandable. Harper, they said grimly, wanted to have a long, heart to heart talk with him, and that too was understandable.

10

THE TOWER BLOCK HELD LITTLE FASCINATION FOR Chesterman and, although this was only his second visit, he was getting a little bored with the place. He was also becoming a little tired of Tarrant and his personal problems, but most of all, he had seen enough of the caretaker to last him a lifetime. This feeling was not shared by the latter who, remembering the two pounds which had already come his way, knew he was on to a good thing.

He greeted Chesterman like a long-lost friend, a warm smile appearing on his narrow face. 'Hullo,' he said, 'haven't seen you since the day before yesterday. Still working on the same case, are you?' He stood up and pushed the ladder-back chair towards Chesterman. 'You sit on this,' he said, 'and I'll squat on the desk.'

Chesterman gingerly lowered himself on to the rickety wooden chair and looked round the tiny office. Every inch of the wall facing him was covered in cheesecake; girls in bikinis, girls in the buff, girls in bras and pants, blondes, brunettes, redheads, green-eyed, blue-eyed and brown-eyed, girls with pouting lips and overdeveloped bosoms, girls flat as planks and all of them shared one thing in common—they were unattainable as far as the caretaker was concerned. One look at him, one whiff of his foul breath, and they would run a mile.

He leered at Chesterman and said, 'Like my pop art?'

'I've got some of my own.' Chesterman reached inside the breast pocket of his jacket. 'Six of them, to be precise. Who do you fancy?'

'Bit on the small side, aren't they?'

'Head and shoulders.'

'Like a passport photo?'

'Similar.'

'I like them full length.'

'Don't we all,' said Chesterman, 'but beggars can't be choosers. Do you recognise anyone?'

The caretaker arranged the pictures in his hand and studied them carefully. 'This to do with that divorce case you were talking about last time you was here?'

'Our client is having trouble with his wife—she intends to contest the action, so we have to be sure that the evidence against her will stick.'

'I'll have to go to court, will I?'

'It might come to that.'

The caretaker searched the photographs again and then scratched his head. 'I'm not too sure,' he said.

Chesterman sighed and extracted a pound note from his wallet. 'Of course you realise we can't pay you to give evidence because that would be very dodgy, but I daresay we would be quite liberal about your expenses afterwards.'

The man plucked the note out of Chesterman's hand and, in exchange, handed him one of the photographs. 'That's the one who spent the night with Major Tarrant.'

Chesterman said, 'Thank you, you've been most helpful.'

'What happens now?'

'Nothing until you hear from us again.'

'Will it be all right to go on my holiday next month?'

Chesterman retrieved the other photographs and walked towards the door. 'I doubt if it will come to court this side of Christmas,' he said.

Chesterman left the tower block without regret and telephoned Wray from a public call-box in the Wandsworth Road.

He said, 'I've just been having an interesting conversation with our friend—we've come up on the numbers game. The woman he picked out is a Mrs Barbara Lee Waterman—a divorcee. She was transferred to Bath early in March of this year. Do you want me to follow it up?'

Chesterman could hear Wray chewing on the stem of his pipe as he considered the problem. 'No,' he said eventually, 'I think Harper will want to look into that angle. You'd better come back to the office; I've no doubt that, once he's spoken to Bath, he will be in touch with us again.'

Wray's assumption was not entirely correct. After Harper had spoken to the Personnel Supervisor in Bath, he was in touch with quite a number of agencies. Barbara Lee Waterman, it transpired, had started her holidays on Saturday, the day before David Tarrant was kidnapped; they understood she was touring the Continent with a friend.

The Sappers of 83 Corps Engineer Regiment had to wait until the CID had finished their detailed examination of the track and the adjacent area before they could begin to raise the sunken Land-Rover, and this recovery operation itself also posed a number of problems. Before the Land-Rover could be lifted out, it had to be moved closer to the shelf where the crane would eventually be positioned. Frogmen righted the vehicle, carried out an under-water reconnaissance and then anchored a number of pulleys to the floor of the gravel pit.

A Scammel recovery vehicle was driven down on to the lower shelf and its winch gear was strung out, the steel wire hawser being passed through the pulleys before it was shackled to the Land-Rover. In this manner, the Land Rover was drawn by the winch gear along the bed of the pit following the route which the frogmen had selected. It was a slow business, since a number of potholes made it impossible for the vehicle to take a straight path, and in addition, it was constantly being unshackled and the hawser relaid as the Land-Rover passed each pulley in turn.

By early afternoon, it was close enough to the shelf for the Scammel to be replaced by a Coles Crane which then lifted the Land-Rover out of the water and placed it down on dry land. Subsequent visual examination of this vehicle revealed that engine and chassis numbers had been chiselled off and acid had been used in an attempt to finally obliterate all traces of these numbers. Two large packing crates and four suit cases were recovered from the bed of the gravel pit and their contents carefully listed.

James Stroud who had, at last, been allowed to make a statement, merely confirmed what the evidence found at the Coxwold gravel pit had already suggested.

The bedroom, which faced south, was a sun-trap even in the late afternoon. From May through to early September it could be uncomfortably warm on a fine day, and this day it had been exceptionally hot for the time of year with the temperature in the mid seventies. McKee, who was lying on the bed facing the window, still sweated even though he was half naked.

In periods of stress, he prided himself that he had the ability to think calmly and clearly and act decisively, but at the moment there was no need for him to think calmly or act decisively because other people were doing that for him. He had planned the whole thing in minute detail and had rehearsed the principal actors in their parts, but now that the operation had reached the point where, temporarily, he was unable to stage manage events, he was finding it almost impossible to relax and do nothing.

The sound of light footsteps outside his room alerted him, and rolling off the bed, McKee crossed the room and opened the door.

Ruth Burroughs said, 'How clever of you to anticipate me.' She held out the set of reins. 'Look,' she said, 'I've finished my sewing, does it meet with your approval?'

McKee took the reins and examined the canvas pouches which had been tied to the leather harness.

'I made fourteen pouches, that was the number you asked for, wasn't it?'

He placed the reins on the chest of drawers. 'You've made a good job of it,' he said.

A faint smile hovered on her lips. 'Aren't you going to ask me in?' she said softly.

His eyes took in her bare feet and the nylon dressing-gown worn loosely over a strawberry pink slip. 'Where's Paul?' he said.

'Golfing. I told you he always goes to the club on a Thursday —remember?'

She was standing very close to him now and their knees were almost touching. She put an arm around his neck and kissed him with an open mouth and gently but firmly pushed him back into the room.

'This is foolish, you know that, don't you?'

'Do you really think that Paul and I will stay together when this is over? I'm going to leave him.'

'I'm not interested in your future plans.'

'Are you also an empty husk like Paul?' Her hand moved across the flat of his stomach and then caressed him. 'No,' she said, 'I can feel you're a real man.'

'You're a whore,' he said angrily.

'Why don't you treat me like one, then? Or are you afraid of what Paul might say or do? He won't do or say anything because he'll never know.'

Her active hand continued to excite him and her body moved against his. The smile was an open-ended invitation, and slipping her arms out of the dressing-gown, she allowed it to fall to her feet. He reached out and tearing off the thin satin straps, he rolled the slip down to her waist with about as much affection as he would have given to peeling a banana.

She stepped back a pace and removed her bra. 'You're an animal,' she whispered, 'a wonderful, savage animal.'

McKee cupped her breasts in the palm of each hand, and then, quite deliberately, he pinched the nipples between finger and thumb.

'You hurt me,' she moaned. 'You really hurt me then.'

McKee stooped, lifted and threw her on to the bed. 'Isn't that what you've been wanting me to do?' he said.

Her teeth were clenched together and the smile on her face was predatory. 'Oh yes,' she whispered, 'you know that's what I want.'

There was no tenderness, no expression of love, just the urgency of a dog coupling with a bitch on heat. They rolled, fought, bit, twisted and crushed one another like frenzied animals cooped up in a cage until, finally, McKee pushed her away and lay exhausted on his back breathing heavily.

She lay beside him in silence, her hand resting on his thigh, and slowly his eyelids began to droop, and seeing this, she leaned over and sought to arouse him.

McKee pushed her hand away. 'What's the matter with you,' he said, 'haven't you had enough?'

She laughed softly. 'Didn't you know?—we Poles have passionate natures.'

McKee turned, his left arm flailed in a half circle and he struck her across the face with the open palm and her skull cracked against the headboard. Four livid fingermarks began to leave their imprint on her cheek and tears gathered in her eyes. McKee grabbed her by the throat. 'I'll kill you,' he hissed. 'I'll kill you if ever I hear you say that again.' He put a foot against her hip and shoved her on to the floor. 'Get out of here, you whore,' he said tightly.

She crawled across the room on her hands and knees gathering the torn slip and bra, and then she managed to stand up, and the tears were streaming down her face and she was trembling like a leaf, and she pushed her blonde hair out of her eyes and somehow she succeeded in composing herself, and there was even a certain amount of dignity about her.

'At least I know who and what I am,' she said quietly, 'but

can you say the same?' She walked out and the door slammed behind her.

McKee rolled over on to his back and stared up at the ceiling. She had posed a question which he had difficulty in answering and for the first time in years, he was in doubt. He closed his eyes; images of the last thirty-one years passed in a kaleidoscope.

It is Saturday, the 28th of June, and the dirt road leading east is a shuffling stream of refugees, stragglers and deserters. Every bus and lorry had been commandeered by the army and only the lucky ones have some form of transport—a bicycle or a horse and cart. Most people are on foot, and the dust rises in a choking grey-white cloud and attacks your eyes and throat, and you are tired and thirsty and very hungry.

Minsk is a long way behind and you have crossed the Berezina, but the Dnieper still lies ahead of you and you will cross it at Mogilev before swinging north-east to Smolensk. You are pulling a handcart on which your mother has placed her treasured possessions and she is walking beside you, a rather stout woman whose ankles are badly swollen, and you are gradually dropping back in the column because she cannot walk as quickly as you would wish, and you think about your sister Svetlana who is married to a doctor and who lives in Smolensk, and you wonder about your father who is a Brigade Commissar with V. I. Kuznetsov's 3rd Army at Grodno, and you hope he is still alive.

And because you are lost in thought, you do not hear the strafing ME 109s until you see the strike of their cannon-shot on the track, and miraculously you are unharmed, and you turn to your mother but she is lying in the ditch by the roadside, and her eyes are already glazed because one leg has been blown off at the hip. But you do not weep because you are numbed with shock, and you abandon the cart and go on, and later, much later, it seems to you that the column is hardly moving at all, and then the reason for this log jam becomes clear.

The road block is manned by internal security troops of the NKVD who are sorting the deserters and stragglers out from amongst the dense column of refugees. For the first time you are aware of the man at your side and you notice that he is trying to conceal the sleeves of his jacket and instinctively you know that he has removed the tell-tale insignia of the red star and hammer and sickle of the Political Commissar, and thinking of your father, you are suddenly disgusted and you wonder if you should tell the troopers. But the NKVD men are observant, and the man is taken into the field and stood apart from the ordinary soldiers, and his hands are tied behind his back and then he is forced to kneel down, and you can see that his shoulders are quivering and the tremor ends only when he is shot through the back of the head with a bolt-operated Moissim Nagant rifle. And suddenly you are afraid for your father and you hope, oh how you hope that a like fate does not await him, but you will never know. He is just one of two hundred and ninety thousand men who will be taken prisoner when the 3rd and 10th Armies trapped inside the Bialystok pocket capitulate.

It is the sixth day of the Great Fatherland War of the Soviet Union. You are Andrei Kalinine and you are fifteen years old.

The city is a scarred mountain of rubble softened by the winter snow. The buildings which are still standing are but empty shells, and their fire-blackened walls are stark in the light of a November morning. You are crouching with the rest of the company behind the rubble of an apartment block, waiting to cross the start line and the objective is the Tractor Works. The city is Stalingrad and this is your first battle.

You are dressed for winter in white hood, white smock and white trousers and you clutch a PPSH machine carbine in your gloved hands, and you have had only eight weeks' training and understandably you are a little nervous and you wish now that you hadn't lied about your age. The platoon sergeant frightens you, but only when he is drunk, because when he is drunk he likes to boast of the things he has seen and done. You recall him telling you that the Fascists had been forced to issue new pay books to their flame-thrower troops in an effort to disguise their trade in case they were taken prisoner, and innocently you had asked why this should be necessary, and the sergeant had smiled wolfishly and said, 'Because we fry them with their own flame-throwers.'

And now Commissar Vatutin is moving along the ranks, and he gives you a warm friendly smile and you feel encouraged, but as he passes you the smile is wiped from his face and he looks stern as he stands before the two men who had been attached to your company from the punishment battalion. These men are dressed in summer uniform and they are unarmed, and they seem more like scarecrows than soldiers, for they are hollow-eyed and despair is written in their faces. Commissar Vatutin draws his Makarov pistol and reluctantly they get to their feet, and climbing over the pile of protective rubble, they start moving towards the tractor Plant. They cover fifty metres before they are caught in enfilade by the MG42 sited in the basement of what used to be the bus depot. The machine-gun stutters briefly and they die twitching in the snow, and the platoon sergeant says, 'They did a good job, that MG could have done the lot of us,' and suddenly you know the sergeant is right.

The rain beats against the canvas roof of the field hospital and the wind, lifting the tent flaps, causes the oil stove to flicker. The ward is paved with duckboards which have become greasy and you are quite sure that the bed is gradually sinking into the glutinous mud. Your right leg is in plaster but you count yourself lucky that it is only fractured and that the pieces of metal from the Shoe Mine have not so lacerated the tendons as to cripple you for the rest of your life. The nurses have done their best to make the ward tidy because Sokolovsky, the West Front commander, is to visit the hospital, and you are feeling particularly proud because you are to be decorated with the Order of the Red Star and the Medal for Battle Merit. The Medal for Battle Merit has been awarded for your part in the liberation of Smolensk on the 25th of September 1943, and you are not sure that you really deserve it for many others in the company who ran through the minefield to attack the strongpoint in the Collective Farm were equally brave and yet they have not been singled out. Perhaps you have Commissar Vatutin to thank for that; he has looked after you like a son since that first battle in Stalingrad ten months ago, and it is not entirely coincidental that you and he stayed together when the 421st Rifle Division was broken up and its survivors sent as reinforcements to 10th Guards Army. Your hand seeks and finds his note which you keep under the straw-filled mattress and you read it once more.

You have never considered transferring into the NKVD before but Vatutin wishes to recommend you and he points out that you will be better able to serve the Fatherland, and as a member of the Komsomol, it is your duty to do so, and you think that perhaps this is what your father would have wanted.

The month is July and the war has been over for two months and you are a Lieutenant in the NKVD screening the returning prisoners of war. They arrive in cattle trucks and when the doors are opened you find that some men have gone to elaborate lengths to commit suicide and you come across one man who has tried unsuccessfully to garrotte himself with a sleeve torn from his shirt. And you place the 9-mm Makarov pistol against his head and squeeze the trigger, and you think nothing of it for you have seen the tattooed blood group under his arm and you know that this swine has served in the Waffen SS, and he is not alone—there are thousands of like bastards who deserted in '41 and '42 and joined the Wehrmacht. Special vigilance is needed to unmask these traitors to the Fatherland, and excelling at it, your work is recognised by the award of the Medal for Valour. This medal, which was instituted on the 17th of October 1938, will do more to further your career in the State Security Forces than any other single factor.

In 1951, at the age of twenty-five, you are sent to the School of Languages to study English for two years, and one day, quite by chance, you run into your sister Svetlana outside the GUM store in Moscow and at first you do not recognise her for she is like an old woman. You learn that her husband was captured in the early days of the war and Svetlana was sent to a forced labour camp for nearly three years under Order Number 274 of 1941. It seems to you that she is looking for sympathy but you remember that when Stalin's son Yakov, an artillery captain, was taken prisoner in Belorussia in 1941, he had no hesitation in imprisoning his daughter-in-law and what was good enough for Stalin's daughter-in-law was certainly good enough for Svetlana. She tells you that her husband never returned from the war and she is living now with a construction worker. She is all the family you have left but you part outside the GUM and you never write or see her again.

In late 1953 you are sent to Kazanakov in the Urals. It is a curious town where only English is spoken and there is a branch of Lloyds Bank and the sole currency in use is English. You were Captain Andrei Kalinine, holder of the Order of the Red Star, the Medal for Valour, the Medal for Battle Merit, the Defence of Stalingrad Medal, the Medal for the Capture of Koenigsberg and the Medal for Victory over Germany during the Great War of the Fatherland, but as soon as you step off the train at Kazanakov you cease to exist.

The question is answered. You know who you are and what you are—you are Andrew McKee, aged forty-six, single, born of British parents in Argentina and by profession you are an insurance broker, and you are about to bring off the coup of the century.

II

T
HEY CAME BACK ON AN AIR FRANCE CARAVELLE BECAUSE
that was the first available flight, and Harper sent a car
to meet them at Heathrow. Tarrant sat between Drew
and Vincent who were ominously silent as they took the M4 out
of London. Neither man told him where they were going and he
was not inclined to ask. He sensed their hostility and although
he could understand the reason for it, he didn't care. He had
given David a few precious hours, and Tarrant hoped that
somehow the time gained would be used to advantage. They
followed the line of the Thames Valley out to the stockbroker
country and then, just outside Goring on Thames, they left the
main road, drove along a lane for about a mile and then turned
into a private drive which led up to the isolated house.

The house had once belonged to the Ministry of Agriculture
and Fisheries until Harper had acquired it on behalf of his Department in 1962, since when it had been used as a country
retreat for guests of the Department, some of whom came will-
ingly, some of whom did not. The basement of this house was
reserved for recalcitrant visitors and, in its way, was rather
unique. Dimming facilities and ultra-violet light made it possible to so regulate the passing of time that a man could quickly
become disorientated. The temperature could also be raised and
lowered at will.

It was sparsely furnished with a steel-topped table, a pair of tubular steel chairs and a steel bunk with biscuit-shaped horsehair mattresses. Every item of furniture in the room was fixed to the floor with six-inch screws. A telephone stood on the table and outwardly there was nothing remarkable about it, except that anyone using it was connected to an exchange in the adjoining room, above which a digital display computer would record the sequence of the numbers dialled and so enable the monitors to make the correct response. It was to this room that Tarrant was brought under escort and then left to face Harper alone.

Harper said, 'I do hope you aren't going to be difficult.'

'Am I under arrest?'

Harper considered the question carefully. 'Not yet,' he said.

Tarrant said, 'I'd like to call Colonel Mulholland.'

'How refreshing—I thought you might want to talk to your solicitor.'

'Can I use this phone?'

'Of course, that's what it's there for.'

Tarrant dialled 01-930-9400 and the numbers flashed up on the digital display. Drew allowed the phone to ring for precisely half a minute and then ordered the fake operator to answer.

A woman's voice said, '9400, which number do you require?'

Tarrant said, 'Extension 5911, please.'

There was a brief pause and then he heard the ringing tone and the number went on ringing and ringing until the switchboard operator said, 'I'm afraid there is no answer from that extention, would you like to speak to someone else?'

Tarrant said he didn't and hung up.

'I expect Mulholland has left the office,' Harper said helpfully. 'After all, it is a quarter past seven.'

'I could try his home number.'

'Please do, I'm in no hurry.'

Tarrant dialled 100, waited, and then said, 'Cherstone 91568.'

'Cherstone 91568. What is your number please, caller?'

Tarrant checked the number displayed on the instrument and said, 'Goringvale 266034.'

There was a pause of a minute or so and then he heard a blipping sound and the operator said, 'Sorry, caller, your number is engaged. Would you like me to call you back later when it's free?'

'Yes, please do that,' said Tarrant.

'You know,' said Harper, 'I find you a curious person, Tarrant.'

'Oh?'

'In your position, I would have asked to speak to my wife. I'd want to know if she'd heard anything more about our son. But you didn't, and I think that is strange.'

'And I think you're pretty strange too. I was brought to this place and the attitude of your goons suggested that I was under arrest, so what did you expect me to say?—Good evening, Mr Harper, have you heard from my wife? For Christ's sake, if there had been any further news of David, you would have told me about it. I was brought here because you want to know what happened in Paris.'

'I know what happened in Paris—I lost half a million pounds' worth of diamonds, and you set the whole thing up. You arranged to have your son kidnapped.'

Tarrant stared at him in disbelief. 'You've got to be joking or else you're mad,' he said.

'I know you did it, and I'll tell you how. You used four men dressed as paratroopers, but James Stroud saw only one of them, and this man was an officer, and apparently he said something about using the airfield as a DZ.'

'A Dropping Zone?'

'Precisely. That's good psychology because, you see, every mother warns her child about speaking to strangers, with the possible exception of policemen, and I think perhaps soldiers are in the same category as far as the child is concerned. At any rate, what more natural place to find a paratrooper than at a deserted airfield where he proposes to hold a practice descent for his battalion. Certainly David would accept that explanation and the man would be able to get very close to those two boys without arousing their suspicion. He knocked both boys unconscious and they were then placed in two packing crates and taken by Land-Rover to a gravel pit just outside Coxwold, where tyre marks would seem to indicate that there were two or three other cars waiting for them. Plaster casts have enabled the police to identify two of these vehicles; one was a Ford Zephyr towing a horse-box and the other was a Mini. I should add that the Land-Rover and the army uniforms have been recovered from the bottom of the gravel pit.'

'What about my son?'

'Well, presumably, you had him removed to a safe hiding-place, and perhaps before very long you will be good enough to tell us where it is and then, some of us at least, can go home.'

'You're fucking crazy,' Tarrant said angrily.

Harper shook his head sadly. 'You disappoint me, Tarrant,' he said, 'I expected reasoned argument from a man of your intelligence.'

'Jesus Christ, that's bloody marvellous coming from you. You've been mouthing rubbish from the moment I arrived here.'

'I can make out a case against you.'

'Charge me then, if you think you can make it stick.'

'Don't be in too much of a hurry. I'm prepared to take all the time in the world if I think it's necessary. The man who set this up knew a great deal about the composition of the General Purpose Intelligence Committee and the financial resources of certain Government departments, and that man could be you. This man is also something of an expert on psychological warfare—he set out to condition us by deliberately killing two men in cold blood for no apparent reason so that when we hear your son's voice on tape we unquestioningly believe that the boy is being tortured.'

'Are you implying that David wasn't tortured?'

'I think he was, and that's what sickens me about you.'

'Christ, what sort of monster do you think I am? We lost our daughter mangled under a Leyland truck, and that boy is all I have left. If anything should happen to him, I don't think I'd want to go on living. There are no limits to what I will do to get him back unharmed—*it's about bloody time you realised that!'*

Harper ignored the outburst. 'You asked for half a million pounds in diamonds and a bill of sale, which perhaps you thought might make possession of those stones quite legal. It was also arranged that you should take the diamonds to Paris where you gave Drew and Vincent the slip according to a pre-arranged plan, met your contact and then handed over the merchandise. I don't have to elaborate any further, do I?'

'I suppose I got this lump on the back of my head because I banged it against a wall?'

'We call it window-dressing,' Harper said imperturbably. 'I've seen more impressive wounds.'

'All right, so I deceived you and they got the diamonds, but I had no choice. They are killing my son an inch at a time, and they will go on doing that unless I continue to co-operate with them.'

'And they told you where and when to give Drew and Vincent the slip in Paris?'

'Yes.'

'Before you left London?'

'Yes.'

'But not, I suggest, by telephone,' Harper said blandly. 'You see, we bugged your phone.'

Tarrant said wearily, 'They sent me a tape through the post.'

'Where is this tape now?'

'In my flat, but I wiped it clean.'

'Because they told you to do so?'

'Yes. Christ, I know it looks bad, but that's the way it was.'

'I shouldn't worry about that,' Harper said in a silky voice, 'it wouldn't have impressed me overmuch if you had been able to produce the tape. I could still argue that it was a put-up job.'

'I bet you can even explain why I didn't attempt to escape when I had the opportunity to do so.'

'Oh, come on, Tarrant, you're not that stupid. You didn't want to spend the rest of your life running from the police.'

Harper propped both elbows on the desk and leaned forward. 'You really are a bit of a shit, aren't you?' he said conversationally. 'You hire two men for the job through the Contractor, both of whom you butcher to put the wind up me, and then finally you liquidate the Contractor just in case he should become talkative. We believe at least five other people are involved and all we want from you are some names and addresses.'

Tarrant said, 'And how about a bloody motive?'

'Greed—and a woman.'

'Alex? Now you really are insane.'

'Not, not Alex. The woman we have in mind is a Mrs Barbara Lee Waterman.'

Tarrant stared at Harper, his mouth dropped open and then slowly closed. 'I hardly know her,' he said thickly.

'Well enough to sleep with her.'

'What?'

'She was seen leaving your flat early one morning.'

'It happened only the once.'

'That we know of.'

'If you don't believe me, why not ask her?' Tarrant said angrily.

'I wish we could, but she's no longer in this country; allegedly, she is on holiday. We know she caught the Dover–Ostend car ferry on Saturday, nearly twenty-four hours before David was kidnapped, but since then we've been unable to trace her movements.' Harper stood up and walked to the door. 'But we are still looking for her, Tarrant, and you know the reason why. We are almost certain that she has the diamonds. Think about that while you're alone.'

The secret eye of the television camera high up in the ceiling spied upon Tarrant and his every move; every reaction was observed on the monitor screen in the adjoining room where Drew and Vincent were watching. Harper gave it a passing glance as he entered before he spoke to the girl seated at the telephone exchange.

'I congratulate you,' he said, 'you were very convincing. How

did you manage to disguise your voice on the second occasion?'
Harper already knew the answer but he liked to give the impression that he was interested even in the most minor details.

The girl smiled warmly, patted her hair and said, 'I spoke through a filter, sir.'

'How clever,' he murmured, 'I would never have thought of that.' He rubbed his chin thoughtfully. 'I don't suppose you could make me a cup of coffee, Miss ...?'

'Runciman,' she said. She stood up and gave him another warm smile. 'I'll make you one with pleasure, it won't take me more than a minute or two.'

Harper sat down in an armchair, waited until they were alone, and then said, 'Well, Vincent, you've been watching him, what do you make of Tarrant?'

'He was ice-cold to begin with but towards the end you had him rattled.'

'But not badly enough to cough?'

'He won't break easily.'

'So?'

'We bend his mind a little,' said Drew. 'Look, we kill the lights, leave him there in the dark, and then push the noise level up until he thinks the top of his head is about to lift off. He won't be able to stand it for long because he's in poor condition. He was complaining about a headache on the return flight and he had the stewardesses feeding him coffee and aspirins from take-off to landing.' He saw Harper shaking his head and tried a different approach. 'Or if that doesn't meet with your approval, we might try psycho-chemicals.'

'That doesn't meet with my approval either.'

Vincent lit a cigarette. 'I wonder if we've got the right man after all,' he said.

Harper looked at him sharply. 'I hope we have,' he said, 'by God, I do. He's the only candidate we've got at the moment, and I'd settle for a straightforward crime any day of the week. If he is innocent, we've got problems, and I don't know where to look for the answers.'

'So we'll have to find his weak spot and make him crack.' Vincent glanced at the image on the screen. 'He hasn't moved from that chair. I think he looks agitated—perhaps he really is worried about his son.'

'If he is,' said Harper, 'we haven't got a case.'

Drew said, 'We don't seem to have very much on his wife— maybe we should ask Special Branch to do a little digging?'

'We'll get nothing more from them.'

'Well, let's try a little aggro on the separation angle. I'll soften him up for Vincent. What do you say?'

Harper said, 'It might be worth a try. She's a very attractive woman and I think he's still half in love with her, but you'll have to play it very carefully.'

'I can handle it,' Drew said complacently.

Drew was a confident young man, full of ambition, who was not given to underestimating his own ability. He walked into the interrogation room, sat down in the chair facing Tarrant and ignored him while he pretended to read through his notebook. Occasionally, he would look up and stare at Tarrant as if seeing him in a different light.

Quite suddenly, and without any preamble, he said, 'When do you plan to divorce your wife?'

'What business is that of yours?'

Drew leaned back in the chair, pushed a lock of fair hair out of his eyes, and with a visible effort assumed a languid tone of voice. 'I don't think you quite realise the seriousness of your position,' he said.

'Oh, but I do. I've been brought to a place not of my own choosing, where I am held against my will and where I am being asked a battery of stupid questions by a berk with a phoney accent like you.'

Drew managed a tight smile. 'I've asked you precisely one question,' he said.

'An irrelevant one.'

'I disagree. We know you have been having an affair with this woman Barbara Lee Waterman, and she's not the sort of woman who sleeps around. According to our information, you two were quite serious about each other.'

'Balls.'

'Am I to take it from that remark that Barbara Waterman is in the habit of sleeping around, or that you were not serious about her despite seeing her frequently?'

'Who told you that?'

'Your caretaker. According to him, you said, "Will I see you for lunch as usual?" or words to that effect.'

'We sometimes had lunch together but there was nothing permanent about our relationship.'

'She was just a casual screw?'

Tarrant said, 'You've got a mind like a sewer, she's not like that at all. She did once stay the night with me, and I think both of us regretted it afterwards. Don't ask me to explain how it happened, it just did. We'd been to a New Year's Eve ball and we came back to my place for a drink and one thing led to another.'

'You knew her well enough to get the tickets in advance?'

'It didn't happen that way. She asked me to go with her because her partner had to let her down at the last minute.'

'Well, I don't blame you for going with her, she's an attractive woman and, in your place, I would have done the same. After all, why should you remain a monk when your wife has been playing around?'

'What the hell do you mean?'

Drew feigned surprise. He was something of an actor and his performance was very convincing. His voice matched the visual expression. 'She works part-time for Friedmanns, doesn't she? As a story consultant for which she earns a pittance.'

'Why don't you get to the point?'

'The point is that she is a very, very close friend of Peter Richardson, their publicity manager—you know what I mean?' Drew smiled and wagged his head as if he were privy to some guilty secret. 'Richardson's had it away with her more than once in the back of his Triumph 2000.'

The knife went in deep and Tarrant rose up out of his chair and drew back his right fist.

Drew smiled easily. 'That really got under your skin, didn't it?' he said. 'Maybe you do care about her after all.'

Tarrant sat slowly down again. 'What do you care?'

'You may have lost a child but that isn't the whole reason for the bust up, is it?'

'No.'

'Your mother-in-law doesn't like you very much, does she? Perhaps she thinks you married Alex for her money?'

'Something like that.'

'How do you get on with her father?'

'Not too well. Alex had a brother who was with the 18th Division which arrived in Singapore just in time for the surrender. He went into the bag and died of beriberi in Changi Jail two years later. The army isn't popular in that family, and I'm a convenient whipping boy.'

Drew stood up. 'Keep on like that,' he said, 'and you'll have our sympathy if nothing else.'

'What happens now?'

'You wait,' said Drew. He walked out and locked the door behind him.

Before he became the middle man, Silk had been a sleeper, and a sleeper must of necessity be something of a schizophrenic. He had been a convinced Communist from the age of eighteen, but acting on orders, he had left the Party shortly after the Hungarian uprising of 1956, since when, outwardly at least, his political viewpoint had moved steadily towards the right. In the General Election of 1970, he let it be known that he had voted Conservative for the first time in his life. To strengthen his cover, he had joined the Territorial Army and Volunteer Reserve in 1960 and was now a troop sergeant in the Yeomanry Reconnaissance Regiment. For a total of sixteen years he had remained dormant, but on Friday, 14th January 1972, he was activated by the District Controller and assigned to an operational cell code-named 'Drabble' to act as the cut-out between McKee and Julyan.

From Sunday onwards, in the interests of security, he was kept in ignorance of McKee's whereabouts and was dependent on both men contacting him. Of Julyan he knew even less, and if by chance they had met in the street, Silk would have been unable to recognise him. At seven-thirty this Thursday evening his wife answered the call from Julyan and told Silk that a Mr Drabble wished to speak to him.

Conscious that she was within earshot, he said, 'Good evening, Mr Drabble, what can I do for you?'

'It's about that sample bottle of Hungarian Riesling you sent us. Of course, neither of us has had a chance to taste it yet, but my wife tells me that she's heard from friends that it's very good and so I'd like to confirm my initial order.'

'I'm out of stock just now, Mr Drabble, but I'm expecting a call from the sales rep at any moment.' Silk hesitated momentarily and then said, 'Tell you what I'll do—I'll get him to drop a note in your box telling you when to expect delivery.'

'Thank you,' said Julyan. 'When might I expect to hear from you?'

'Tonight.'

Julyan said, 'I must say you give a very good service.'

'We try to,' said Silk and hung up.

The call from McKee came through a bare five minutes later and Silk was on hand to answer it.

McKee said, 'Any news?'

'We've got a firm order for the Riesling. The customer is anxious to know where and when.'

'Can you get a message to him tonight?'

'Calvert can drop it into his box.'

'All right then, tell him it's the Lounge Bar, the Grand Hotel, Northampton, seven-thirty tomorrow night. He is to wear his identification badge and we'll use the agreed contact procedure.'

Silk said, 'I suppose this will mean something to him?'

'It will.'

'What about us?'

'I want you and Calvert parked outside Croft's sweet shop in Towcester at two-fifteen tomorrow afternoon. About fifteen minutes later Tarrant will arrive in his Ford Zephyr UVY 421H. Shall I repeat that number?'

'I've got it—UVY 421H.'

'I hope you haven't written it down.'

'I'm not stupid.'

'Good. Tarrant will be taking a call in the telephone booth across the road from the shop. As soon as he's finished and left the immediate area, I shall want to speak to you in the same phone-box.'

'I understand.'

'One more thing, will that woman of yours make any trouble?'

Silk smiled at his wife across the room. 'Janet's going to her mother's for the weekend,' he said, 'she won't mind a bit.'

12

JARMAN ARRIVED IN ST MALO A FEW MINUTES BEFORE SIX and checked in at the Hotel Central in the Grande Rue. He asked for a single room with a private bathroom and was offered one on the second floor overlooking the street, which he promptly accepted. He registered under the name of Marcel Vergat, confirmed with the receptionist that he could stay on until the following Monday and then went up to his room.

Jarman closed the French windows which opened on to a tiny balcony overlooking the narrow cobbled street, drew the blinds and locked the door before he started to unpack. Tarrant's briefcase lay on top of the clothes, and he wished now that he had got rid of it *en route* and just kept the velvet bag which contained the diamonds, but, at the time, he had been reluctant to stop and find a secure hiding-place for it. He hung up his suits in the wardrobe, left a clean shirt and a fresh change of underwear on the chair and put the rest away in the chest of drawers. Loosening the cord around the neck of the bag, Jarman tipped the diamonds out on to the bed, and having sorted them into eight piles roughly equal in size, he then filled the pouches on the money belt. He took the belt with him into the bathroom, stripped off, showered and then dressed for dinner. He checked his appearance in the full-length mirror and satisfied himself that the receptionist would have to be particularly observant to notice that his waist-line had become a little thicker in the space of an hour.

The dining-room was a European melting pot. A party of six Italian nuns held silent court at one table with their Mother Superior whose facial expression clearly showed that neither the group of German students who were loud in voice and spirit, nor the young French couple who held hands while they fed each other with delicate slices of lobster met with her approval. She appeared to make an exception where Jarman was concerned, for every time their eyes happened to meet, she favoured him with an acid smile. Deep in thought, he returned her smile vacantly.

Jarman was thinking about Melissa Julyan and wondering how far he could trust her. Until this moment, he had dealt all along with professionals whose competence he respected, but now he was being forced to deal with an amateur and his security would be at risk. He had never been totally enthusiastic about this operation from the time it was first mooted in Berlin, but he had been ordered to do it by the KGB, and if you were a Russian it paid never to argue with those people. He remembered that evening as if it were only yesterday.

He had left his hotel in the Linden Allee and walked briskly towards the U Bahn in Theodor-Heuse Platz and the savagely cold January night had turned his escaping breath into a white cloud and the frozen snow had crunched under his feet. At least on the U Bahn he had been able to thaw out a little, but it was only temporary, and the cold night air pierced through him like a knife as soon as he left the station at Zoologischer Garten. He had an appointment to keep with a man called Max and he'd crossed the busy Budapester Strasse opposite the Kaiser-Wilhelm Church and they had met outside the Berliner night-club and he had been surprised to see that Max was accompanied by a woman.

The night-club had proved expensive—three half-litres of beer had cost Jarman forty-eight marks, but Max had explained that this was a cover charge for the floor show and that the next round of drinks would not be so costly. And he had thought it was typical of headquarters to let the man in the field foot the bill, and they had been shown to a table for three in a tiny booth off to one side where he could only see the cabaret if he looked into the angled mirror on the wall because he was sitting with his back to the stage, but of course Max had made sure that he had a clear view, and that too was quite typical of the people from headquarters.

And he had found himself hypnotised by Max's bloated face and had watched those thick, full lips opening and closing like the mouth of a codfish as the words softly tumbled out, but those pale expressionless eyes were never on him, and the plump blonde woman at his side just sat there passively and Jarman thought that she was an extraordinarily bovine creature with about the same intelligence as a cow.

And the lights had gone down and Max had stopped talking because it was impossible to make himself heard above the noise of the taped music and besides, his eyes were now riveted on the floor show which Jarman could only see in the mirror. The sketch had consisted of two girls; one, a Nigerian, was dressed as a maid, while the other, a dark-haired girl with a creamy skin, had worn a white satin evening dress and elbow-length matching gloves. The maid had helped her to undress in time to the music and it had begun tastefully enough but, in true Germanic fashion, it had turned a little coarse and suggestive towards the end, and he had found the psychedelic lights trying on his eyes and all he could see was a couple of blurred forms performing a ballet on the bed. And suddenly he had become aware of the cramp in his right leg, but when he had tried to move, his kneecap had caught the pedestal supporting the table and a wave of pain had shot through his body. And Jarman had been forced to sit through the whole of the first cabaret as one dreary, boring routine followed another and he had grown hot and sticky, and the acrid, stale tobacco smoke had nauseated him and the black, vinyl-covered bench seats had begun, with the passage of time, to feel as though they were made of iron.

And as the outline plan was unfolded, Jarman had questioned the whole concept, and then the woman had suddenly come to life, and her eyes had bored right through him, and her voice had been no more than a low hiss but she'd spoken of a soldier's duty to obey orders and he had been left in no doubt that the line had been drawn. He recalled that they had left the Berliner at eleven-thirty and he had walked with Max and the woman as far as the Bristol in the Kurfürstendamm, and when they had parted there, the woman had said, 'I expect that, after all these years, you must be pleased at the thought of going home?' And he had managed to smile but that was all.

Jarman finished his coffee, wiped his mouth on the napkin, smiled once more at the Mother Superior and left the dining-room. He collected his raincoat, and leaving the key to his room at the desk, walked out of the hotel.

In the height of summer, the narrow streets of the old Corsair city were always crowded, but this early in the season he could walk unhindered along the pavement and the cafés around the Place Chateaubriand were half empty. He went on past the floodlit Hôtel de Ville and, crossing the cobbled road by the slipway, entered the dark flight of steps which led up to the ramparts. A fresh breeze was coming off the sea and he turned up the collar of his raincoat, but it afforded him little protection and he wished that he had worn a heavier suit. He walked slowly along the ramparts listening to the waves slapping against the wall some fifty feet below, and in the distance he could see the lights of Saint Servain and it suddenly came home to him that, within the space of a day or two, he would be leaving France never to return, and all because one man wanted six and a half million francs as a down payment for services about to be rendered, and he knew that after years of faithful and dangerous service all he could look forward to was promotion to the rank of Major and a desk job in Moscow. Moscow, he thought, was just as cut off from the rest of the world as was the fort sitting on that piece of rock off the shore, except that, when the tide went out, you could walk across to it and that was more than could be said of Moscow.

The woman, whose headscarf concealed most of her face, was standing in the wall between the gun emplacement and the outer wall of the bastion and was looking down at the harbour mole as if fascinated by it.

Jarman stopped at the next embrasure and lit a cigarette. 'There's a chill in the air,' he said.

The woman turned her head towards him. 'And it comes not from the east,' she said in a low voice.

'Somebody had a poetic turn of mind when they picked that phrase for a recognition signal,' he said. Jarman took hold of her arm and she fell in step beside him. 'I presume you've spoken to your husband?' She inclined her head and the mannerism irritated him. 'Well, did you or didn't you?' he snapped.

'Of course I did.'

'He hasn't changed his mind, has he?'

'He has no reason to as long as you people stick to your part of the bargain.'

Jarman patted his stomach. 'You haven't got any problems,' he said, 'I'm a walking bank. We'll leave early tomorrow morning, right?'

'I thought about eleven.'

'You'd better think again,' Jarman said grimly. 'I intend that we should be in San Remo by tomorrow evening.'

'I have an au pair girl with me,' she said as if that explained everything.

'You've what?'

'I need help to look after the children, they're only four and five and they can be quite a handful.'

He flicked the cigarette end over the ramparts and watched it fall into the dark sea. 'My mother had eight,' he said, 'and she didn't have anyone to help her.'

She jerked her arm away from his. 'We have a straight-forward business arrangement,' she said angrily, 'and it doesn't include a sermon from you. I've told Françoise she can have the weekend off.'

'Françoise?'

'The au pair. I think she has plans to catch the 10:30 bus into Parme.'

'You think,' he said scornfully.

'All right then, I know for a fact that she intends to catch that damned bus. I'll pick you up in my car outside the Casino at a quarter past eleven.'

'We're never going to make San Remo tomorrow.'

'We will.'

'I wish I could believe that.'

'I used to be a rally driver; you can spell me if you're up to it.'

'What sort of car have you?'

'A white Mercedes. Oh, don't look so disapproving—it's four years old.'

She turned and ran down the steps to the street below and he stood there watching her until she turned the corner into the Rue Bidouanne and was lost to sight. Jarman thought she was typical of her class—arrogant and expensive to keep, like most of the yachts in the basin below the ramparts. He wondered how long it would take Melissa Julyan to get through six and a half million francs.

13

MCKEE HUNG UP HIS SUEDE JACKET IN THE HALL, RAN the palm of one hand over his head and smoothed the thin dark hair into place before entering the lounge. Burroughs, a glass of whisky and soda at his elbow, was seated at the writing desk studying the farm accounts, while Ruth was curled up in an armchair apparently engrossed in a book. Neither looked up when he entered the room.

McKee cleared his throat. 'I take it this studied form of indifference is supposed to mean something?' he said.

Ruth looked at him blankly. 'Should we jump to attention, then?'

'I need your help.'

'Really?'

'With the boy.'

Burroughs turned sharply to face him and accidentally knocked over the glass and the whisky formed an ever-widening pool on the desk. 'For God's sake,' he said, 'leave the poor child alone. Hasn't he suffered enough already?'

'Did I say I was going to hurt him?'

'Well, aren't you?'

'No. I want him to record another message.'

'To send to his father?'

'Or his mother,' McKee said evenly. 'Maybe that doesn't

meet with your approval either, Paul? Perhaps you would handle it differently and then we'd spend the rest of our lives behind bars. You've become soft, Paul, that's your trouble.'

Burroughs pulled a handkerchief from his pocket and began mopping up the whisky. 'Ruth will help you,' he muttered, 'I'm busy with these accounts.'

McKee said, 'Of course you are, even I can see that. I'm sure Ruth has no objection to helping me.' He turned and smiled at her. 'Or have you, Ruth?'

Ruth Burroughs uncurled her legs and stood up. 'I'm surprised the question even occurred to you,' she said.

The musty smell came up from the cellar as soon as McKee opened the door. He switched on the light and ran agilely down the flight of wooden steps, Ruth following unhurriedly. He approached the bed on which David lay and noted with satisfaction the look of fear on his face.

'Look at him blinking his eyes in the light,' he said callously, 'he's like a bloody little mole.'

'If you had spent hour after hour in total darkness, I expect you'd blink like a mole too.'

McKee said, 'Are you getting soft too?' He picked up the set of reins which were lying on the top shelf of the wine rack. 'I want you to untie him and get him on his feet while I fix this harness.'

'Do I remove the gag?'

'Not yet,' he said, 'I don't want his blubbering to distract me.'

McKee stooped down and dragged out a battered fibre suitcase from beneath the wine rack. He snapped open the locks, and raising the lid, took out fourteen sticks of plastic explosive which resembled plasticine and smelt faintly of almonds. He squeezed the sticks into shape and carefully slotted them into the canvas pouches on the set of reins and then, having selected a like number of gun-cotton primers, he cut off fourteen lengths of varying size from a reel of Cortex instantaneous fuse; he then married each primer with a length of fuse and plugged the primers into the plastic explosive. Gathering the trailing ends of the Cortex together, McKee secured them with a rubber band before reinforcing them with twine.

The suitcase also contained a tin, and unscrewing the lid, he gingerly removed three fulminate-of-mercury detonators which he rigged to a push–pull switch. For safety reasons, and because he saw no point in taking unnecessary risks at this stage, he kept the explosive harness away from the push–pull switch. When the two parts were ultimately joined together, he planned to attach twenty feet of trip wire to the switch.

McKee sat back on his haunches and rubbed his chin thoughtfully. 'How's the boy making out?' he said.

'His fingers are in a mess.'

'What?'

'The burns are oozing pus.'

'Put some antiseptic on them then and bandage them up.' She moved towards the steps. 'Not now,' he said, 'later, when I've finished with him.'

'You enjoy hurting people, don't you?'

'I don't get any pleasure from it, but sometimes it is necessary.'

'As when you hit me, for instance?'

'Yes, much as I regretted doing it.'

'Is that an apology?'

'No,' said McKee, 'just an explanation. Now hold the boy still while I slip the reins over his shoulders.'

'You're turning him into a living bomb, aren't you?' she said.

'Yes. You see, it's a form of insurance. About an hour ago, I left a message for Harper with Mrs Tarrant. I think he will meet all our demands because it will give him the chance to get close to us and so I am preparing a little surprise for him.' He looked at David and smiled thinly. 'We're going to record another message for your mother,' he said. 'You'd like that, wouldn't you?' There was no response from the boy but McKee was exasperated to see that he was close to tears. 'I don't want to hear a sound from you when Mrs Burroughs removes the gag.

Understand?' David nodded his head, blinking rapidly. 'Good; and mind you don't forget it, because if you give me any trouble, I'll light a cigarette and burn you some more.'

Tarrant lay on his side, a hand cupped to his face shielding his eyes from the fierce lights in the ceiling. The biscuit-shaped mattresses on the bunk felt like planks of wood beneath him, and although he was not a stranger to living rough, a too active mind and a splitting headache made sleep impossible. He knew that the seeds of distrust which Drew had tried to plant in his mind would take root and multiply like cancerous cells unless resisted. It was possible that Alex was having, or had had, an affair with a man called Richardson, but Drew had struck a false note in the telling of it. There was nothing cheap or furtive about Alex and even in the wildest moments of fantasy, he couldn't imagine her making love to anyone on the back seat of a car.

It was part of their technique to undermine a suspect, to make him feel alone and unwanted, and although he could recognise it, Tarrant couldn't deny that it was beginning to work in his case. Harper wanted him to accept the fact that if any love and trust had survived their separation, it was now being steadily eroded and eaten away.

They'd had twelve years togther and it hadn't all been bad, and until Sarah had been killed, enforced separation had strengthened, not weakened, the bond between them. Sarah's death was the cataclysm and he knew now that he should have asked for a compassionate posting, but there had been so much bitterness and recrimination, that Aden with all its troubles had seemed more welcome. If he had been a little more perceptive, he would have realised that Alex, who was on the verge of a breakdown, was trying to exorcise a misplaced sense of guilt, and he'd had to wait until now to discover that blindingly simple fact. And he recalled what Alex had said yesterday in the stillness of David's room—'I was going to meet her, I usually did you know, but it was my birthday and you telephoned me from Aden just as I was about to leave, and but for that I would have been there on time.' And instead of trying to comfort her, he'd sought to explain it rationally. For three years she'd lived alone harbouring a sense of guilt, and Christ, it would have been a miracle if she hadn't looked for love and comfort elsewhere. There was a gap between them and it was getting wider, but it could be bridged if he made the effort, and he could make a start by talking to Alex about Sarah, and perhaps it might help if he acknowledged that he was mostly to blame for the break up of their marriage, and then somehow he would have to find the right words to tell Alex how much she meant to him, and that shouldn't be too difficult because these last three years had been damned empty without her.

Vincent said, 'Daydreaming?'

Tarrant swung his feet off the bed and sat up. 'I didn't hear you come in.'

'I tread softly.'

'And talk softly too?'

'When necessary.' Vincent sat down at the table and opened his notebook. 'There are one or two points which I should like you to clear up,' he said.

Tarrant came and sat across from him at the table. 'Like what?'

'You're a second-grade staff officer in Colonel Mulholland's section?'

'You know I am.'

'How long have you been in post?'

'Eighteen months—it's a two-year posting.'

'And in that period the General Purpose Intelligence Committee would have held something like seventy-eight meetings?'

'We do meet once a week.'

'Approximately, how many have you missed?'

'Not more than half a dozen.'

'So by now you must know everyone quite well?'

'For the most part they are just casual acquaintances. Faces change with individual postings, and you never really get close to someone you only see once a week for an hour or so.'

'Tell me what happens at these meetings.'

'Harper must know, he attends them regularly.'

'I'd like you to tell me.'

'We assemble in the Main Building every Tuesday morning shortly before ten. Coffee is available for those who want it and then the meeting starts promptly...'

'Do you take coffee?'

Tarrant stared at Vincent and then, after a moment's hesitation said, 'Quite frequently.'

'And naturally you stand around and chat to people?'

'Yes.'

'What about?'

'This and that—the weather, the news, the cost of living, sport and so on.'

'Did you ever talk about David?'

'Only when someone asked after him.'

'Who?'

'Crompton; he met David when we were stationed in Germany.'

'Who's Crompton?'

'A second-grade officer in MI10.'

'Did you ever mention David's school to anyone?'

'I'm not sure. Perhaps I may have done so, I know some people were always comparing their schooldays with their sons. I probably said my bit.'

Vincent tore a sheet from his notebook and placed it in front of Tarrant. 'I want you to list everyone who is a member of the General Purpose Intelligence Committee,' he said, 'and then I'd like you to put a plus sign against those people with whom you regularly converse, a minus sign against those to whom you occasionally speak and a zero against those with whom you're only on nodding terms.'

Tarrant said, 'What do you hope to achieve by that? To highlight those who make a point of seeking me out?'

'Something like that,' Vincent said guardedly.

The plus signs would not necessarily be a true indication, the zeros could be equally revealing, either because Tarrant had something to hide or because the man who was using him as a front had taken good care to stay in the background. Vincent watched him closely to see if there was an instance of noticeable hesitation when Tarrant applied gradings to names, but could detect none.

Tarrant gave him the completed list. 'I hope this is what you wanted?' he said.

The question was to remain unanswered because Harper chose that moment to walk in and there was something about him which seemed to convey a sense of urgency and purpose to Vincent. He assumed rightly that Harper was going to take over and he phrased his question accordingly.

He said, 'Do you want me to remain, sir?'

'You may as well,' said Harper. He waited for Vincent to give up his chair and then slid into it. 'It seems your friends are anxious to stay in touch with you, Tarrant. We've had another message from Drabble. The tonal quality isn't very good because it has been re-recorded over a land line.' Harper's knee sought the silent buzzer under the table. 'But apart from a certain fuzziness, it's quite audible.'

In the adjoining room, Drew, seeing the flash from the signal light, put the Grundig on playback and pushed the sound through to the interrogation room. Simultaneously, a second Grundig was switched to record.

The phone rang and a male voice said, '9984.'

'This is Drabble, I have a message for Major Tarrant.'

'He isn't available.'

'Mrs Tarrant?'

'Why do you want to speak to her?'

'Don't stall me. I'll call back in five minutes and you'd better make sure she is there to answer.'

The phone rang again and Alex answered it.

Drabble said, 'Mrs Tarrant, I want you to hear this and make sure it gets through to Harper. We want to go to Brazil in a VC

10 and I don't plan to go to the airport in a bus. Harper will arrange to collect us in a Wessex Helicopter which will then land alongside the VC 10, and the only reception committee I want to see is a WRAF Air Quartermaster from Transport Command. Stay by the phone, Mrs Tarrant, because I will be calling you again in a few minutes.'

The tape ran on for a few seconds and then the male voice said, 'The first call was timed at 2110 hours and the second at 2119. Trace procedure proved negative.'

The third call was timed at 2135 and Drabble took the conversation up almost as if there hadn't been a break in it.

He said, 'The RAF can work out the details of the flight plan to Brazil, but I'm selecting the departure airfield for the VC 10, which is to be on standby from 1500 GMT tomorrow, Friday. I shall also tell them where to position the Wessex helicopter and I'll give the pilot his course. I need a Sarbe beacon to guide the Wessex in on to the landing site and recognition panels to mark the pad. We'll indicate wind direction with a home-made smoke pot. This is going to be a one-way trip, so we don't want the Foreign Office fouling things up because those Brazilians have got to welcome us with open arms. Your husband will deliver the beacon and the panels, and when I call you tomorrow between eleven and eleven-thirty, I want to hear his voice on the line, and I expect to get confirmation that everything is lined up and ready to go. Understand?'

'I think so,' Alex said faintly.

'I hope you do, because if anything goes wrong, I plan to blind your son.' His voice dropped to a low hiss. 'And believe me you'll have proof that I'm not bluffing.'

The tape ended, cutting short a high-pitched scream.

Tarrant said, 'Christ in heaven, was that Alex?'

'I'm afraid it was,' said Harper, 'but she's all right now. You have my word for it.'

'What does that count for?' Tarrant said bitterly.

'At least as much as yours does.'

Tarrant rubbed his forehead. 'Are you going to meet his demands?'

Harper avoided his eyes. 'Supposing there is a defector,' he he said evasively, 'and the opposition has agreed to a transfer fee of half a million pounds. Wouldn't it be safe to assume that he means to divulge information which would imperil the safety and security of this country and put countless lives at risk?'

'What are you driving at?'

'Surely, as a soldier, you must realise that we can't bargain with the enemy merely because he has a hostage.'

Tarrant leaned forward. 'I know this,' he said fiercely, 'that as a soldier I have an unlimited yet unwritten liability. In an extreme case, that liability means putting my life at risk, but I have yet to meet anyone who supposes that this liability also extends to my son. If you are toying with the idea of detaining me so that you can have a free hand to bluff it out with Drabble, I should forget it because you've still got Alex to reckon with.'

'I'm not entertaining any such idea, you will be free to talk with Drabble tomorrow.'

'Talking means nothing unless we do as he wants.'

Harper said, 'We might run to the beacon and the recognition panels, but can you see the Combined Chiefs of Staff sanctioning the use of a Wessex and a VC 10? Can you see the Foreign Office clearing it with the Brazilian Government?'

'I can, if you ask them.'

'As an act of mercy?'

'Yes.'

'Oh, come on, Tarrant, they have an obligation to fifty-five million other people besides your son.'

'You want a more positive reason? I'll give you one—this is the first chance we've had to get close to Drabble. What's to stop you putting a snatch party inside the Wessex? Or why not ring the VC 10 with snipers and pick them off as they transfer from the Wessex?'

Harper folded his arms behind his head and leaned back in

the chair. 'You know,' he said, 'I rather like the idea of using a few skilled marksmen.'

'The safety of my son comes first.'

'Naturally.'

'What happens now?'

'Vincent will run you home while I fix everything up.'

'I'd like to speak to Alex.'

'Of course, please use the phone.'

'Does that trick thing actually work?'

'It will when I tell the operator to put you through,' said Harper.

Every word which had passed between them had been faithfully recorded by Drew, and with subtle editing, Tarrant could be held equally to blame for his son's death if anything went wrong.

In the absence of any instructions to the contrary, the CID team investigating the Tarrant affair were still treating the kidnapping as a criminal case. In response to an appeal by the North Riding Police, a number of witnesses had come forward claiming that they had seen a Zephyr or Zodiac towing a horse-box in the vicinity of Coxwold on Sunday afternoon. There was the usual conflict of opinion regarding the registration number and outward appearance of the vehicle, which was variously described as being light blue, aquamarine, sapphire blue and pale green in colour. Sighting reports also came from as far afield as Scarborough, Malton and Easingwold.

However, two rather more promising lines of enquiry were being pursued. Although the labels had been removed from the combat suits, Ordnance (Contracts) Branch at the Ministry of Defence had been able to identify the makers from the type of cloth, cut and stitch pattern. The four suits in question were part of a rush order for ten thousand which had been placed with Keane and Parkinson to back up depleted maintenance stocks. Stock control at Bicester subsequently indicated that issues from this batch had been made to eleven regular and

reserve units in the last three months, all of whom were instructed to carry out a check of these items and report any
deficiencies by 1200 hours on Friday.

The long-wheelbase Land-Rover, which had never been
registered with a licensing authority, was now known to have
been stolen from the security compound of Wallis and Sons in
Acton some four days prior to the kidnapping. Records showed
that Goring, whose past form included car theft, was operating
a legitimate repair service in Hounslow up to the time of his
death, and a search of the premises in Hardinge Avenue led to
the discovery of four empty two-gallon cans of Army Department high gloss green paint. Unfortunately, issues of this lot
and batch number had been made to a large number of units in
the training organisation and the reserve army, and in consequence it was estimated that the stock check would not be completed until late on Friday.

Friday

SIXTH DAY

14

FRIDAY CAME WARM AND CLOSE AND THE MUGGINESS IN the air hinted that, before the day was out, a storm would break. Julyan had spent a restless night with sleep only coming fitfully and he'd lain awake listening to the dawn chorus and the early morning sun had filled the room with light. This day was for him a point of no return, and it was only to be expected that he would experience a certain nervous tension amounting to excitement.

Months of patient planning were about to come to fruition, and somehow the day would have to be lived through as though everything was perfectly normal, and he would cope with the office and just hope that nothing would arise which would detain him beyond five o'clock. It could be no more than a hope because experience had shown that Governments were fond of making awkward decisions after Parliament had risen in the afternoon which had to be implemented over the weekend.

He wondered if he should ring Harper and ask him how the Tarrant affair was progressing but he couldn't make up his mind whether it would seem more natural to ignore the whole business. There was always the danger that, if he showed too much interest, he might invite suspicion and he had no desire to face any more of Harper's loaded questions. He remembered all too clearly how he'd reacted when Harper had cheerfully asked him to name someone who might be worth half a million pounds to the opposition and he had been forced to nominate himself amongst others. Those few minutes on the telephone had given him some anxious moments.

Julyan reached out for the packet of cigarettes on the bedside table; he was not a heavy smoker, but in times of emotional stress, he felt the need of one most acutely. He lit the cigarette and lay back on the pillow again and watched the thin stream of blue smoke drift up towards the ceiling, and thought about Melissa who was so very different from his first wife. Grace had had a placid nature which was just as well, since rheumatic fever in childhood had left her with a weak heart. They'd had four years together before she died and life had been a void for him until Melissa came along. Melissa was young and beautiful and selfish and vain, and passionate and exciting to be with, and she had captivated and made him young again. And she was generous and extravagant and demanding and clever and ruthless, and she was strong, strong in a way which Julyan knew he could never match. Melissa had changed his style of life and opened his eyes to what the future held in store for them if they continued to jog along in the same old rut, and perhaps he might have shrugged it off if it hadn't been for the Hobart Committee with their recommendations for streamlining the service.

Streamlining, he thought, was pure Whitehall jargon to disguise a drastic reduction of the SIS. It implied increased efficiency at less cost and everyone knew that was just a pipedream. Hobart meant that a lot of people would be prematurely retired and Julyan knew for a fact that he was amongst those chosen to be axed. Until that redundancy list had appeared, he'd had every reason to suppose that one day he would be invited to fill the post of Controller, Secret Intelligence Service, because he ran the Eastern European Desk, and there was no more important branch of the Service. But now it seemed that years of loyal and often dangerous work would count for nothing.

For Julyan, the years of war and peace had been equally dangerous. In 1953 he'd parachuted into the Kiev region with a

team of four in order to assess the strength and effectiveness of
the Ukrainian Nationalists. His agents had been carefully
selected from the remnants of Vlassov's Army of Liberation
who had managed to evade repatriation to Russia after the war,
and although they were the best he could find, they weren't good
enough to escape detection. The operation had been a total
failure and only Julyan and an agent code-named 'Paul' had
made it to the Baltic where they were picked up by one of
Gehlen's fast patrol boats.

No one else amongst his contemporaries had been so close to
the firing line since the end of the war and Julyan refused to
believe that that one set-back in an otherwise unblemished and
successful career accounted for his impending retirement. The
truth was that there was a desire to save public money and the
country no longer cared about the guardians of its security. The
message was clear enough—it was every man for himself. Even
though Hobart was still a year away, the idea of pre-empting
the future had been conceived last summer when he'd made
contact with Max through a double agent in East Berlin.

And Max had been very discreet in sending him a travel
brochure, and Julyan had taken the hint and decided that they
would go to Sweden for their summer holiday. There was nothing clandestine about his movements and the office knew where
they could reach him if it was necessary, but some of his associates knowing Melissa's tastes, might have expressed surprise
had they seen the chalet in Lysekil. They had taken the ferry to
Gothenburg and then driven up the west coast through Udde-
valla to Lysekil. He recalled that they had arrived in pouring
rain late on a Saturday afternoon and he had driven to the
Turistbyraen in the market square to ask the way to the chalet,
and the agency girl had phoned for the hostess. The hostess had
turned out to be a plump woman who spoke not a word of
English and knew no other tongue but Swedish, and she had led
Julyan back the way they had come for mile after mile until
suddenly she'd turned off the road and they'd bumped along a
narrow cart track through the dark pine forest which had

eventually opened out into a small clearing. She had left them there after showing them the well and the Elsan latrine tucked away in the woods, and Melissa had been tearful and then angry when she was faced with the prospect of cooking a meal on the two-ring electric stove.

There were two other chalets in the clearing, but although it had only been mid-August, they were apparently already closed for the coming winter. And they had spent two miserable stinking wet days up there alone before Max and his woman had arrived, and nothing had been right for the children because they were a long way from the sea, and when, in desperation, he'd taken them into Lysekil between cloudbursts, there was no beach to speak of in the fjord but only a lido surrounded by jellyfish. And but for Max, the trip would have been a disaster. It had taken Julyan less than six hours to negotiate the contract, and in return for half a million, he'd undertaken to deliver the name of every British agent east of the Oder–Neisse line.

Julyan stubbed out his cigarette, rolled out of bed and in bare feet, walked over to the windows and drew back the curtains. As he stood there looking out over the heath, he calculated the odds and decided they were in his favour. There could be no leak from East Berlin because the double agent had long been dead and safely buried deep within a disused coal mine, and apart from that one meeting at Lysekil, he had avoided seeing Max and relied instead on a dead-letter box for communication which, in fact, had seldom been used once the plan had been conceived. Any member of the Magic Circle knew that, for an illusion to be really successful, the audience had to be distracted; Tarrant was far removed from the pretty girl in a scanty costume and tights, but in a way, he'd served a like purpose.

Harper arrived at the office at much the same time as the duty nightwatchmen were being relieved by the day shift. High on his list of priorities was the need to select and assemble a balanced team for the assassination of Drabble. Faced with the choice of taking them out either as the helicopter came in to the pick-up point or as they transferred from the Wessex to the VC 10, Harper decided to keep both options open for the time being. In adopting the former course, he would require specialists in close quarter combat, for the latter he wanted marksmen.

Drew and Vincent were automatic choices but he reckoned to back them up with a further six men, and for the next hour, Harper went through the card index system until he was satisfied that he had picked the best possible team. During the course of the morning he planned to send the snipers down to Bisley under Vincent, where they would zero their rifles before they moved back to the nine-hundred-metre firing point and really settled down to the serious business of getting their eye in. Although he proposed to leave the final choice to Vincent and his team, he felt sure that they would prefer to use the proven Number 4 Lee Enfield with telescopic sights to the semi-automatic FN, and he rang down to the duty armourer and instructed him to put aside two hundred rounds of competition ·303 ball ammunition. Drew, of course, would want to take his group out to Braintree Hill, but Harper was reluctant to accept such a widespread dispersal of his available manpower and he therefore came to the conclusion that they would have to make do with the pistol range in the basement.

The sudden clatter of the teleprinter in the outer office came as a surprise, for it heralded the arrival of Miss Nightingale, and until then he had been unaware that time was passing so quickly. The signal which she placed on his desk had been originated by Interpol and was addressed to the Commissioner, Metropolitan Police, repeated to Director Subversive Warfare for information. The text read:

YOUR OPS 20 DATE TIME GROUP 171500 ZULU FIRST STOP LUXEMBOURG POLICE CONFIRM THEY HAVE DETAINED MRS BARBARA LEE WATERMAN AND TRAVELLING COMPANION MISS

KATHLEEN GRIERSON STOP WATERMAN AND FRIEND ARRIVED
GRÁAS HOTEL LATE TUESDAY STOP PLEASE ADVISE YOUR
INTENTIONS STOP MESSAGE ENDS STOP.

Harper read it through twice before initialling the signal and
placing it in his out tray. The possibility that Tarrant was involved in the conspiracy was rapidly being excluded as far as he
was concerned, but he supposed that Wray or someone would be
making a trip to Luxembourg later in the day to check out
Waterman, but he personally had lost all interest in the woman.
The identity of the defector both worried and intrigued him but
he had no time to dwell on it. Between nine and a quarter to
eleven, when he left to meet Tarrant, Harper was never off the
phone. He called and was in turn called by the Home Secretary,
the Minister of Defence, the Chief of Air Staff, the Commissioner of Metropolitan Police, Wray, the Director Staff Duties
(Army) and the Joint Warfare Establishment at Old Sarum.
Somehow, he even found the time to brief Drew and Vincent.

Tarrant could sense the atmosphere in the flat as soon as he
stepped inside the hall. Her mother was a brooding presence
and the stiff upper lip expression on her face suggested that she
was already in mourning for David. Behind the rimless glasses
her eyes looked red and he could imagine what sort of effect she
had had on her daughter.

'Where's Alex?' he said.

'Lying down in David's room.' He started to move past her
but she caught hold of his arm. 'She needs the rest, John.' The
'John' bit came out reluctantly.

'Yes,' he said slowly, 'I expect she does.'

'Alex was just about to drop off to sleep when you rang up
last night. I really do think you might have called earlier. She
was very worried.'

'About me?'

The corners of her mouth went down. 'Alex was on tenter-
hooks in case anything had gone wrong in Paris.'

'Nothing did, did it?'

'It was still very inconsiderate of you not to have phoned earlier.'

'Unfortunately, I wasn't in a position to do so.' He tried to get past her for the second time but she still blocked his path. 'Are you planning to spend all morning in the hall?' he said.

'We can't talk in the lounge, there's no privacy in there.' Tarrant looked at her questioningly. 'There's a policeman in there,' she added.

'There has been since Monday.'

She pursed her lips disdainfully. 'What did you say to upset Alex last night?'

'What?'

'She was crying when I went into her room. She wouldn't tell me what was the matter and I think, as her mother, I have a right to know.'

Tarrant said, 'I don't think you've got any right at all, but since you're that curious, I'll tell you. Last night when I spoke to Alex I told her that I loved her.'

'Love,' she said scornfully. 'What do you know about love? Alex could have had a dozen better than you.' The doorbell rang but she ignored it. 'There's Ian Gilmour for one.'

'Who?'

A thin smile of triumph etched itself on her mouth. 'I see you don't know about him, do you?'

The bell rang again and Tarrant opened the door.

Harper said, 'For a moment I thought nobody was at home.' He smiled at Alex's mother and said good morning to her and then strode into the lounge as though he owned the place. 'Where's Alex,' he said, 'resting in bed?'

'Yes.'

'Best place for her,' said Harper. 'There's no point in Alex being present when Drabble calls, it will only upset her.'

Whether it served any purpose or not, Alex made sure that she was present when Drabble called. Five nights with little or no sleep had left her looking haggard and strained and the brown linen dress she was wearing looked several sizes too large for her.

Drabble came through at eleven-twenty and asked to speak with Harper first. He said, 'Do we get the helicopter and the VC 10?'

'We've agreed to your request,' Harper said cautiously.

'And is the Brazilian Government prepared to offer us political asylum?'

'We are in touch with them, I don't think there will be any difficulty.'

'All right, I want the VC 10 positioned at Lyneham ready to take off at 1500 GMT Saturday.'

'And the Wessex helicopter?'

'I'll let you know about that after I've got the Sarbe beacon and the recognition panels.'

'We have to know . . .'

'You don't have to know anything more at this stage, Harper. Now put Tarrant on the phone, I want to speak to him.'

Tarrant took the phone from Harper. It was unnecessary since the amplifier made it possible for everyone in the room to hear what was being said but no one was inclined to make the point to Drabble.

Tarrant said, 'I'm listening. What do you want?'

'How well do you know Towcester?'

'I've passed through it once or twice.'

'This time you'll approach it on the A43 from the South. Just before you come to the crossroads in the centre of the town, you'll see a public call-box on the right-hand side of the road opposite a sweet shop. You be there at 1430 sharp and I'll call you again.'

'Supposing it's out of order?'

'Find another one and call your wife. We'll use her as a relay.'

'I understand.'

'Good. Make sure you use your own car because we'll be looking out for UVY 421H and I'd hate anyone to get clever at this stage. Perhaps this message will help to make the point clear to all of you.'

The message was from David and his voice was a little hesitant but he came over clearly enough.

He said, 'I'm wearing a sort of harness, Dad, which Mr Drabble has made. He tells me it's like the reins mothers used to put on their tiny children when they took them out for a walk, except that it has a lot of pouches sewn on to it and each pouch contains half a pound of plastic explosive. Mr Drabble says there is about seven pounds of PE in all and it will make quite a bang if it should go off.' David swallowed audibly and then went on with some difficulty. 'He's wired them up to a push–pull switch on the back of the belt which goes round my waist, and he's attached a length of wire from the switch to his own body. Mr Drabble says that I am joined to him by an umbil...' he stumbled and then got the word out, 'umbilical cord, and if anyone should try to shoot him or if he was knocked over, the sudden jerk on the wire would be enough to set the charges off.'

'That was very good, David,' Drabble said cheerfully, 'but there were just two things you forgot to mention. When you are in the harness your hands will be pinioned in front of you so that you can't touch any of the wires, and secondly you will be wearing that harness all the way to Brazil. You know what you are, David? You're a walking, talking bomb.'

Alex was the colour of chalk, tiny beads of sweat had gathered on her upper lip and her hands were shaking. No one had to tell her what seven pounds of explosive could do to the human body, there had been any number of photographs in the Press and on television showing the damage done to buildings in Belfast to leave nothing to the imagination. She started to walk out of the room and then broke into a run.

'I think I'm going to be sick,' she gasped. Her mother gave Tarrant a venomous look and then rushed out after her.

Tarrant said, 'What do you propose to do now?'

'Do?' Harper said vaguely.

'You can scarcely use a sniper to pick him off, can you? He's still outsmarting us.'

The duty policeman said, 'He's just made his first mistake, sir. He's never spoken that long on the phone before without a break. We should be able to trace the call.'

Harper looked at the man through narrowed eyes. 'What's your name?' he said.

'Smallwood, sir.'

'Well, if you're that confident, Smallwood, I suggest you check with the GPO to see if they have had any success.'

'I think you're trying to avoid my question,' said Tarrant.

Doubt seethed in his mind but Harper was not going to confide in Tarrant. It was inconceivable that they should tamely surrender, but the assassination of Drabble was no longer a simple matter. A young, innocent life was at stake and he could appreciate the anguish of David's parents, and the trouble was that he had become too closely identified with and emotionally involved with the Tarrants. If he had stayed aloof he could have reached an objective decision, but at this precise moment Harper badly needed advice from someone who was unbiased. In the back of his mind was the thought that perhaps an old friend like Edward Julyan could help him to reach the right decision.

Harper said, 'I'm just beginning to accept the fact that Drabble is going to win all along the line and I find that a bitter pill to swallow.' It was a bland lie but he made it sound convincing.

Smallwood cleared his throat. 'I don't understand it,' he said. He looked embarrassed and uncomfortable.

'What don't you understand?' Harper said icily.

'The GPO have failed to trace the number, sir. They are absolutely certain that it originated in the Kettering area but they can't pin it down.'

'Drabble,' said Harper, 'has been preparing this operation for months and he has used a number of different methods to contact us. It's my belief that he's found a telephone in a disused camp and has tapped it in to the nearest junction box.'

'He's thought of everything.'

'Do I detect a note of admiration in your voice, Tarrant?'

'Far from it.'

'I'm glad to hear it. I presume you will be staying here for the next hour or so?'

'Yes. Why?'

'I'll get someone to deliver the Sarbe beacon and the recognition panels to you.'

'Thank you.'

'Don't thank me,' Harper said irritably. 'Sooner or later that man has got to make a mistake and I want to be in a position to take advantage of it when he does.'

The jacket and trousers of a combat suit are packaged separately each in its own cardboard box sealed with black binding tape. A cursory check of the stores held by B Squadron of the Yeomanry Reconnaissance Regiment by the permanent staff showed that the correct number of boxes was displayed on the shelves, but since the signal had stressed that the stocktaking had to be one hundred per cent, they proceeded to examine the contents of each box. Eight were found to be empty and the size labels matched the suits which had been recovered from the gravel pit.

The NCO in charge of B Squadron clothing store was a Sergeant Silk. Subsequently, when the police called at Silk's private address, they were informed by Mrs Silk that her husband had just left with the advance party to prepare the weekend training camp at Felixstowe for the rest of the squadron. This news had been a surprise to the permanent staff who were not aware that any exercise had been scheduled for that weekend.

15

THE WAITING HAD BEEN THE WORST PART AND, IF THERE was a painless way of killing time, Tarrant wished that someone would let him in on the secret. He had sat with Alex in David's room but they had scarcely been left alone with one another for more than a few minutes at a time because her mother had always found an excuse to intrude upon their privacy.

Alex had been quiet and withdrawn, and in an effort to dispel the brooding silence, he'd asked her about David's books on War Gaming, and she had produced the 20-mm lead soldiers which their son had painted, and until he had seen the Cuirassiers, Chasseurs à Cheval and Grenadiers of the Imperial Guard, which were correct in every detail, he hadn't realised that David was so interested in the Napoleonic era. And as she had catalogued his interests, Alex had taken hold of his hand and held it firmly except when her mother had appeared, for, like an infernal cuckoo clock she had regularly popped in and out to say her piece. And he had been on edge too, because much as he wanted to be with Alex, he was worried that Harper might fail to deliver the items Drabble wanted. Viewed dispassionately, he had no cause for alarm, but at the time, he had been able to think of a dozen good reasons why Harper should cry off at the last minute.

Delivery had been held over until the last possible moment so that Tarrant made the rendezvous in Towcester with less than ten minutes to spare and he lost precious time looking for a place to park the Zephyr in what was a small town crowded with shoppers. He locked the car, checked to see that the boot was secured and then walked back to the phone booth. With a Sarbe beacon and a set of recognition panels in the boot and a Browning 9-mm automatic in the glove compartment, which Harper had thoughtfully provided on signature, he couldn't afford to take any chances.

A plump, middle-aged woman trundling a shopping basket on wheels just beat him to the call-box. In mounting irritation, he was forced to watch her search through her handbag, take out a purse, sort out the small change, drop the purse on to the floor, retrieve it and then laboriously dial the number she wanted. After all that, it came as no surprise when she got the wrong number and had to start all over again. It seemed to him that the conversation was never going to end, and although Tarrant kept looking at his wrist-watch, she was in no hurry to finish. She finally ran out of time and had to hang up, rewarded him with a gracious smile when he opened the door for her, accidentally barked his shins with the shopping trolley and apologised for being so long. He muttered something inconsequential and gratefully slid past her. Inside the box the smell of her cheap scent was overpowering.

He waited, nerve ends jangling, conscious that he was three minutes late for the contact. Tarrant wasn't the only one who was keyed up. The phone rang sooner than he had expected.

Drabble said, 'I have no time for people who cannot follow simple orders.'

'A woman got here before me,' Tarrant said heatedly. 'What did you expect me to do, throw her out?'

'I expect you to make sure that it doesn't happen again.'

'Listen—I've got a Sarbe beacon and you've got my son— now are we going to make a trade or not?'

'Of course we are going to make a trade—eventually.'

'All right,' said Tarrant. 'So what do I do now?'

'You're to go on to Kirby Hall.'

'Where's that?'

'Try looking north-east of Corby.'

'And what then?'

There was no reply and Tarrant repeated the question but all he heard was a faint click as Drabble rang off, and he left the box feeling angry and frustrated.

Unknown to Tarrant, Silk and Calvert had noted his every move and then, having satisfied themselves that he was not being followed, Calvert rang through and reported their observations to Drabble.

Tarrant went on up through Northampton and Kettering and stopped off in Corby to ask the way. Kirby Hall wasn't exactly well known, and in the end he had to go to the TA Drill Hall and borrow a one-inch ordnance survey map of the area before he was able to locate it.

The Hall was over four hundred years old and only the shell of it remained. It had been one of the great houses of the Elizabethan Renaissance, built by Sir Humphrey Stafford in the hope that he might entertain the Queen, but she never came. It had had its moments of glory; Anne of Denmark had stayed there once, and James I actually made three visits, and then two hundred years later it was derelict. Wars had left it unscathed, fire had never touched it, but once the lead had been sold off the roof, time and weather had ravaged it. The Office of Works accepted guardianship in 1930 when it was scheduled as an ancient monument.

Tarrant parked the Zephyr under the trees, paid five-pence admission fee and strolled into the inner courtyard. There were eight other people viewing the ruins not one of whom made the slightest attempt to contact him. A girl in a red trouser suit, whose face was totally obscured by the brim of a large shapeless hat and smoked glasses, did show a passing interest in him, but he thought that might have something to do with the fact that she was hanging on to the arm of a man who looked old enough to be her father, and really the only mystery about them was whether they were husband and new wife, father and daughter or man and mistress.

He spent over two hours in the courtyard and still no one came near him. There were more than a hundred different places which Drabble could have used as a dead-letter box, and without knowing what to look for, it would have taken Tarrant several days to have eliminated them all. He was like a goldfish in a bowl circling aimlessly about, the object of passing curiosity, and it began to dawn on him that Drabble had no intention of making contact. He had been directed to Kirby Hall because its isolation made it easy for them to check that Tarrant wasn't being followed. He had no way of knowing whether Drabble would have set up a fail-safe RV or not, but it irked Tarrant to recall that he had practically suggested it. He went back to the car and drove around until he found a public telephone.

Smallwood answered his call and that surprised him, because although he had no grounds for thinking so, he had expected someone from Harper's department to be on hand.

Smallwood said, 'It doesn't seem to be going too well, sir, does it?'

'Has Drabble made contact with you?'

'Yes, about three quarters of an hour ago. He sounded angry.'

'He was acting—it was a set-up to make sure that I was alone. He may do it again before he takes delivery of the beacon, and I think he'll keep me running until dark. He won't risk a contact in daylight.'

Smallwood said, 'You're probably right, sir. He's set the next RV in Thorpe Langton; there's a telephone-box opposite the church. You are to be there at five-twenty.'

'What was the name of that village again?'

'Thorpe Langton—it's north of Market Harborough. Do you have a map of the area?'

'Yes.'

'You're going to need it,' said Smallwood.

Harper took one look at the cellophane-wrapped beef sandwiches which Miss Nightingale had kindly provided for him and decided that he wasn't really hungry after all. He didn't fancy the glass of milk either but his secretary nursed a theory that it helped to keep a stomach ulcer at bay, and although he'd never felt even the suggestion of a pang before, there was a chance that today could see the start of one, and all because he couldn't arrive at a decision.

The more he thought about it, the more he became convinced that the helicopter was Drabble's blind spot. He was counting on it to pick his people up at a given spot at a given time, but if the Wessex went unserviceable and had to back off at the last minute, then all the hostages in the world wouldn't help him to overcome that hurdle. Such a last-minute hitch might not throw Drabble but he wondered if the rest of the team were as resolute; a set back at that precise moment might well crack their morale and then Drabble would have his hands full holding them together, and if he was so distracted, then the risk to David's life would be diminished accordingly. Harper made a mental note to cease referring to him as David. The use of his Christian name made for emotional involvement and he had to remain detached and aloof if he was going to see the situation in its true perspective.

He knew that in the end he would have to refer the problem to the Minister of State but when he did, Harper wanted to be able to so advise him that the final decision would go his way. At the moment, it certainly wouldn't because the scales were tipped one way. The only certain factor was that a boy stood to lose his life and the reverse side of the coin was anyone's guess. The Minister would insist on an accurate assessment of the danger to national security and Harper could only hazard a wild guess, and in those circumstances the Minister would naturally go for what amounted to a sell out.

He buzzed Miss Nightingale and asked her to connect him with Edward Julyan. Sometimes a person who was not close to the problem could see things with a clearer eye, and what better person to consult than an old acquaintance holding a similar position to his own?

The phone rang, and answering it, he heard Miss Nightingale say, 'You're through,' and then Julyan said, 'Good afternoon, Cedric, to what do I owe the pleasure?'

Harper said, 'Let's go to secure speech.' He pressed the button on the scrambler, waited for a second or two and then said, 'It's the same old problem, I'm afraid.'

'Tarrant?'

'In a way. I can nail Drabble and the defector but the boy may well be killed in the process.'

'Do you know who the defector is?' Julyan said calmly.

'No—if I did, there would be no problem. I'd grab him before he had the chance to join up with Drabble. My quandary is should I risk a boy's life on the assumption that a bigger issue is at stake?'

Harper waited for an answer, and the break in the conversation seemed to go on and on. 'Are you still with me?' he said quietly.

'Yes, I'm thinking,' said Julyan. There was another pause, shorter this time, before he said, 'In your place, I would dump the problem in the Minister's lap; it should be his decision. I'm sorry not to be more helpful but that is the only advice I can give you.'

'Two heads are better than one,' Harper said vaguely, 'and at least you have confirmed my own view of the situation. Thank you for listening so patiently.'

'It was my pleasure,' said Julyan.

Harper replaced the phone and sat back in his chair. Idly, he picked up the scrap of paper on which Tarrant had listed those on the General Purpose Intelligence Committee whom he knew in varying degrees. In view of what had happened since Sunday, it was ironic to see that amongst those graded as virtual strangers were Poppleton, Julyan, the Director of Naval Intelligence and himself. His eyes went to the clock on the wall and he drew some satisfaction from the knowledge that there was no pressing need as yet to approach the Minister and he decided to wait and see what happened. It was hardly an inspiring policy but it had its points.

McKee's little army was beginning to muster slowly but surely. Now that Silk and Calvert had joined him at Hillglade Farm, only the man known to McKee by the code word 'Drabble' remained at large and he, of course, was the key figure, for without him the whole enterprise would become a barren and sterile affair. They were approaching the crucial stage when their security would reach its lowest point and they would become vulnerable. In less than three hours McKee and Julyan would meet face to face for the first time ever, and all the weeks of careful planning and preparation would come to fruition only if Julyan had the nerve to go through with it. In his own mind, McKee was satisfied that until now, he personally had left nothing to chance. The risks had been calculated before each stage of the plan had been implemented, and only in the matter of procuring the arms and the explosives had they been treading on dangerous ground.

The plastic explosive had been obtained from French Army sources during the previous February and, following a short visit to Paris during the Easter holiday, had been smuggled back to England by Calvert lashed to the chassis members of his car. Part of the consignment had been earmarked for the total destruction of Goring and Findon while the remaining seven pounds had been stored at Hillglade Farm. The acquisition and storing of the small arms had posed a number of security problems, since unlike explosives, they were not only harder to come by but were also easier to trace through the registration number stamped on the breech of each weapon. Rather than approach an Arms broker direct, Jarman, acting on instructions, had placed an order with the contractor and later, Silk had collected the merchandise from a safe drop and had stored them at his place until they were required.

They had taken care to ensure that at no stage had the defector been placed in jeopardy and McKee could only hope that the same consideration had been shown to them, because they were as good as dead if the man had been stupid enough to attract the attention of the British Security Services. It was the one phase of the operation over which McKee had no control, and knowing this, he drank a little more of Burroughs' whisky and tried to relax while he waited for the phone to ring.

It rang some twenty minutes later just as he was beginning to think that something had gone terribly wrong.

Ruth Burroughs said, 'It went off very well. He spent about two hours looking round the Hall and then Paul spoke to him on the telephone at Thorpe Langton a few minutes ago.'

'How did he sound over the phone?'

'Paul said he seemed agitated.'

'Good. If he stays worried he will do as he's told.'

'Do we come back now?'

McKee checked the time. 'Yes,' he said, 'you do that.' He planned to keep Tarrant running for a while longer yet before he allowed Calvert and Silk to make contact with him. He thought it unlikely that Harper had fixed a bleeper to the car because there was no evidence that Tarrant was being followed, but he intended to make quite sure. He finished his whisky and then went up to the bedroom to change.

McKee opened the chest of drawers and picked out the striped tie. It was, he thought, typical of Max that he had elected to tweak the English over their inbred sense of snobbery and beyond doubt, it was the most improbable recognition signal he'd ever used. It was ludicrous to think that success or failure now rested on two men who would be wearing similar ties when they met. McKee would never have believed it if his instructor at Kazanakov had told him that a day would come when he would wait for a man to approach him in a crowded bar and ask if he too was a member of the British Ski Association.

He could see fat Max now, his face gashed in a broad smile as he briefed him on the recognition procedure, and the snow had been falling heavily as the light faded from the slopes, and below them in the valley the lights of the village of Thalkirchdorf were burning, and then Max had taken off, his skis kissing the snow as he hurtled downhill towards the warmth and comfort of the Gasthof Trauber, and his mocking laughter had hung in the stillness of the pine woods. McKee had no love for the Germans but for fat Max he nursed a lasting hatred. Even if they did originate from the KGB, taking orders from a Bavarian upstart made him want to vomit.

16

TOURS, CHÂTEAUROUX, MONTLUÇON AND ROANNE WERE behind them now. They had covered more than three hundred and sixty miles but they still had another three hundred and eighty to go before they reached San Remo, and although they had averaged seventy-two miles in the hour, Jarman knew that they would have to do better than that once they got on to the motorway at Lyon. They would get a good clear run down to Aix-en-Provence, but as soon as they started to move across through Cannes and Nice, their average would drop off sharply.

There was nothing wrong with the way she drove, but according to his calculations, they would be lucky if they crossed the frontier much before midnight, and he wished to avoid that. He had tried spelling her at the wheel but he had been forced to recognise that he could not match the mileage target which she had established. It seemed to Jarman that a bond existed between the woman and the car and that she was able to push the Mercedes to its limit and yet remain in complete control. If it hadn't been for the children they would have made even better time, but Melissa Julyan had insisted on stopping for lunch, and subsequently, both children had kept on asking to go to the lavatory because they had drunk so much Coke with their food that it was damn nearly running out of their ears.

The weather had also been against them, and for over an hour they had driven through a violent thunderstorm with the rain pouring down from a leaden sky, and that had been particularly nerve-racking because the wipers had failed to keep the windscreen clear, and since it was a right-hand drive, she relied on him to say when it was safe to overtake. Latterly, with the weather improved, the needle had been flirting with the hundred mark, and yet, such was her road sense and ability to anticipate hazards that Jarman had not felt at all nervous.

She sat upright, her hands at ten and two o'clock on the wheel, and the strength in her small-boned wrists was self-evident as they went through the tight bends on Route National 7 between Roanne and Tarare. Her mouth was set in a straight line as if she was determined to ignore the shriek of tyres sliding across the surface of the road, while mind, eyes and limbs worked together in perfect co-ordination. Her right foot touched the brake as the car came into each corner and then stabbed back to the accelerator at just the right moment. The smell of hot engine oil was strong inside the car and the late afternoon sun beating in through the glass turned the interior into an oven which not even the draught coming from the lowered side windows could lessen. Half drugged by the heat and the fumes, both children now slept fitfully on the back seat.

Jarman loosened his tie and unbuttoning the shirt at the neck, used a handkerchief to wipe off some of the sweat which had gathered in the folds of his throat. He envied the woman's apparent coolness and he wondered how she achieved it; it could not be entirely due to the fact that she was not wearing a bra beneath the silk blouse, and fascinated by the sight of the erect nipples on her breasts, he stared at her in open-mouthed admiration. Women usually provoked a low key response but this one attracted him strongly. There was a quality about her which suggested that she was beyond the reach of most men, and seeing her in profile, he could well understand how Julyan had become so completely infatuated that ordinary standards of morality no longer applied and no act of betrayal was too monstrous if it succeeded in pleasing her.

The worst part of that section of the road between Roanne and Lyon was behind them now and they were closing fast on L'Arbresle, and he wondered how long she would be able to keep it up before she showed signs of fatigue. The constant drumming of the tyres and the heat of the engine had a hypnotic effect on Jarman and he fought unsuccessfully to keep his eyes open. His head lolled forward on to his chest and presently, only the restraint of the seat belt held him upright, and when at length she spoke to him, her voice took on a muzziness which failed to penetrate.

Sharp nails cruelly pinched the flesh on the back of his wrist and the shock pulsated the adrenalin through his veins and aroused him. He half turned in his seat to strike out and then checked the instinctive movement when he saw the narrowed, contemptuous eyes staring at him through the polaroid sun glasses.

'You're a clod,' she hissed vehemently, 'a stupid, lazy, good-for-nothing clod. I went past a truck back there completely blind because you had fallen asleep. I know you are not much good as a driver but at least you can try to stay awake.'

There could be, and there was no excuse for his laxity, and although he knew that she was in the right, Jarman still seethed with anger. This domineering, over-confident, arrogant woman was no better than the whores around the Boulevard Madeleine, and it was on the tip of his tongue to say so when he saw the caravan looming up in front of them. He shouted a warning, and as she swerved out into the centre of the road, he saw too late that they were on a collision course with a Citroën Safari which had just overtaken a slow-moving Simca.

They were less than fifty yards apart and there was nothing anyone could do. Melissa stamped on the brakes and her whole body was arched back against the seat like a drawn bow. The wheels locked and the agonised, screaming tyres left pieces of burning rubber upon the surface of the road. For a split second Jarman had a clear view of the other driver and saw the panic in his bulging eyes and was convinced that he could hear him screaming.

They met head-on at a combined impact speed of one hundred and seventy miles an hour and the radiator disintegrated and the engine block, torn from its mounting, was pushed back through the forward bulkhead at an oblique angle. Travelling upwards, it severed Jarman's right leg and driving through his rib cage it churned his trunk into a bloody and obscene pulp. Simultaneously, the windscreen exploded like a bomb and a piece of metal from the facia panel sliced through his scalp and entered the brain.

The frame and chassis members buckled and were compressed into a solid mass of useless metal; the offside stub axle was wrenched off and the wheel, bursting through the mud-wing, soared up into the air, and then falling back, it bounced on the tarmac and then trundled drunkenly into the field bordering the road.

Melissa Julyan was frozen to the steering column which, becoming a blunted lance, entered her stomach and with relentless energy bored right through her slim body until finally the shaft reappeared between her shoulder blades. The doors sprang open as if plucked by giant hands and a small figure was tossed out into the roadway where it lay inert.

Locked in a fatal embrace, both cars now slewed across the road so that the oncoming Simca caught the rear end of the Citroën a glancing blow to lift it up and over on to its roof which in turn crumpled like a piece of tin foil. The driver of the Opel Rekord braked hard but the weight of the caravan behind pushed the car forward and in slow motion, it gradually approached and then finally hit the Mercedes. The impact smashed the headlamps of the Rekord and forced open the boot on the Mercedes and fuel from the ruptured petrol tank began to form a dangerous, fast-spreading pool on the tarmac. The cacophony of tortured metal and inhuman screams were a long time in dying.

The driver of the Opel was the first to reach the shattered

heap of wreckage and the sight of the mangled bodies inside the Mercedes so unnerved him that he reeled away vomiting. It was quite apparent that the adult occupants were beyond help but a child, trapped between the bucket seats up front and the bench seat at the back, was still alive. The first car to approach the scene of the accident was a Volvo travelling towards Roanne out of Lyon, and finding the road ahead blocked, it turned back and alerted the police in the next village. It then took just over ten minutes for a Citroën ambulance car from the First Aid Post in Tarare to arrive, and it was joined shortly afterwards by two police cars and another ambulance, but until the fire tender and recovery vehicle appeared, the combined efforts of the police and the ambulance men failed to extricate the five-year-old girl trapped inside the Mercedes. Even then, it was necessary to lay a carpet of foam over the road to counteract the potential fire risk of the ruptured petrol tank before the rescue work could begin.

Crowbars were used to prise the seats apart, but despite the greatest care on their part and the tranquillising effect of the morphine injection, the child screamed as she was lifted clear and placed inside the ambulance. After that, it was simply a butcher's job. An acetylene torch was used to cut through the steering column which impaled Melissa Julyan in her seat and once this was accomplished, it was comparatively easy to remove her lifeless body. Any victim of a road accident looks ghastly even if the resultant injuries are only superficial and violent death was no stranger to these firemen and recovery mechanics from Lyon, but they required an absolute detachment of mind when they started to free the broken hulk of what had once been a man. They ripped off both doors, cut out the supporting pillar, and having burned a hole through the roof, they were able to lift the engine block away from Jarman's lap with a crane. Devoid of all emotion, they then moved on to the Citroën Safari and started on the grisly task of removing the decapitated body wedged inside the overturned car.

Bundled inside four black plastic bags, the bodies were

eventually taken to the morgue where, as a formality, they were pronounced dead on arrival. Tentative identification was made on the basis of passports, driving licences and other documents recovered from the scene of the accident and at seven-thirty that evening, the British Consulate was notified of the deaths of a Mrs Melissa Julyan and her son, Mark Clifford, aged four, and they were also informed that her daughter, Elizabeth Anne, aged five, was on the D.I. list.

The police were able to supply the presumed address of the next of kin from the information contained in the International Green Card issued by the General Accident and Assurance Exchange Corporation in respect of a 1968 Mercedes 220 SE with the registration number TLA 0934 C, and the Consulate was requested to notify those concerned and arrange for positive identification. Similar action was taken in respect of the American citizen Walter J. Outram whose body had been recovered from the same car, but in his case the authorities were anxious to know why he was wearing a money belt which contained a number of uncut diamonds valued at approximately six and a half million francs.

17

THEY RAN TARRANT RAGGED, SENDING HIM FROM ONE RV
to another just as he knew they would. They even
compelled him to put the Zephyr up on a ramp to check
that a bleeper had not been attached to the chassis, and the
mechanic at the wayside garage had thought him a crank when
Tarrant had insisted on getting into the inspection pit with him
to check on a supposed oil leak from the sump. Thereafter, his
route had followed no recognisable pattern, and if marked on a
map, would have resembled the scribbling of an infant child.

Night had fallen when he drove into the car park of the Cross
Keys. His headlights picked out a bold sign on the boundary
fence which said 'Coaches Welcome'. It seemed that the pub
was popular; he counted eighteen other cars parked in the yard,
but then it was the only sizeable roadhouse on that stretch of the
A607, and it was close enough to Leicester to draw trade from
the city. Tarrant thought that Drabble had picked a good venue.

Wall to wall carpeting covered the floor of the lounge bar,
easy chairs were grouped around low coffee tables, a line of
evenly spaced, plastic-covered stools faced the bar and diffused
wall lighting gave the room an intimate atmosphere. Tarrant
perched himself on one of the vacant stools, ordered a whisky
and soda and prepared himself for a long wait. His instructions
were clear enough; he was to stay there until he was contacted.

Looking around the room, he saw that there were three quite separate groups; everyone else had come in a party, he was the odd man out. He wondered if the contact would arrive alone.

He picked up a copy of the *Leicester Mercury* which someone had left on the bar and scanned every page, but of course he could find no mention of David, and there was no reason why there should be. Public interest in the continuing search for a missing boy had waned after a day or two and as far as the Press was concerned there had been no new developments. Drabble had wanted it kept out of the papers, which suited Harper, and Tarrant had had no say in the matter, but now he began to wonder whether it had been such a good idea after all. It occurred to him that, as Harper did not have to contend with public opinion, he could handle the situation whichever way he chose, and that did not necessarily mean that he would have David's interests at heart. Tarrant put the paper to one side and ordered another whisky.

An hour went by without anything happening except that he chain-smoked his way through five cigarettes, and then he began to wonder if they had left a message, but the barman had nothing for him and so he went outside to check on the Zephyr which he found was still in the same parking slot. He tried the doors but they hadn't been tampered with and it became perfectly obvious that no one had been near the car. He hung around for ten minutes or so, during which time several more cars arrived, and then, weary of the whole business he went back inside and ordered a third whisky and a couple of cheese sandwiches to go with it.

The lounge bar gradually filled until it was standing room only, but not one person in that bar took any notice of Tarrant. Waiting was a demoralising business, and although he knew it was intended, he wished they would get it over and done with. He kept glancing towards the entrance hoping against hope that something would happen.

Suddenly, something did. The woman sitting on the next stool knocked his glass over.

The man with her said, 'My God, that was careless of you, Ruth.' He flashed a smile at Tarrant. 'I hope it missed you.'

'There was only a drop left. No harm was done.'

A cool hand touched his. 'I'm dreadfully sorry,' she said, 'let me get you another drink.'

'No, really, it's quite all right.'

'Please,' she said, 'I'll feel awful if you don't.' Her voice was soft and pleading and it bore just a trace of an American accent.

Tarrant smiled back at her. 'Well, if you insist,' he said, 'I'll have a ginger ale.'

'Why not have something stronger?'

'I'm on the limit now.'

'Ah yes,' she said, 'we can't have you in trouble with the police.'

She was, he thought, in her early thirties, although it was hard to be sure. She had a long, fine-boned face which ended in a narrow chin, but the blonde hair did much to soften her features. She was wearing a stone-coloured leather suit over a black sweater and she was sitting with one leg crossed over the other. Her thighs were worth a second glance. He noticed that she was wearing a platinum wedding ring but he very much doubted if the man she was with was her husband. Looking at her, Tarrant thought she could have found someone better.

The man flashed him another smile. Nicotine had stained his teeth a dull yellow. 'I haven't seen you here before,' he said.

'I'm just passing through.'

He pushed the glass of ginger ale towards Tarrant. 'Going to London?' he said.

'Yes.'

'Thought so.'

'Why?'

'Your accent gave you away.'

'It always does.'

The man raised his glass. 'Cheers,' he said.

The salute marked the end of their brief conversation and Tarrant didn't blame him. If their positions had been reversed he also would have concentrated all his attention on the woman. He toyed with his ginger ale, not really wanting it, but as long as he was forced to sit there waiting for a contact, it was a harmless enough drink to while away the time.

A man behind him said, 'Hullo Ruth, what a surprise seeing you here. Where's Paul?'

Tarrant glanced sideways at the woman sitting beside him to see how she reacted to being caught out with another man and he had to admire her composure. She took it all in her stride.

'You know Paul,' she said, 'he's busy talking to his friend in Johore Bahru. I don't think you've met Steve, have you? He's spending the weekend with us.'

The mutual introductions started because the newcomer had arrived in a party, and Tarrant caught the names of Burroughs, Calvert and Scotson amongst others. A small crowd gathered and he began to feel in the way. He sat there for about fifteen minutes trying not to listen to their conversation, but it was difficult not to do so, and in the end, he left the bar and played the fruit machines until he ran out of small change.

He didn't see the Burroughs–Calvert–Scotson party break up, but when next he looked their way, they were no longer there, and he saw that there was only a quarter of an hour to go before closing time. He checked with the barman again to see if there had been a message for him, but as he had half expected, no one had called. It occurred to him then that perhaps they had a duplicate set of keys, and that while he'd been sitting in the pub, they had calmly helped themselves to the gear he'd locked away in the boot. Tarrant went outside again to check on the car.

He had figured that they would try to pull a fast one but it still came as a bit of a shock to find that the Zephyr had been lifted. He felt more than a little sheepish when he walked back into the bar and asked if he could use the phone. The landlord wasn't too keen on the idea but then the pound note caught his eye and that changed his attitude.

Smallwood answered the phone and he sounded irritable.

He said, 'About time. What kept you?'

All day long he had been taunted by Drabble and his friends and he had had just about enough. 'Who the hell do you think you're talking to?' he snapped.

Tarrant heard him swallow and then Smallwood said, 'I'm sorry, sir, I thought it was the station with news of my relief. We've gone on to a twelve-hour shift system and he's overdue.'

'Had any other calls?'

'One from Drabble about half an hour ago. Mr Harper would like to speak to you about it, sir. You can reach him at his office.'

'At this time of night?'

'So I understand,' Smallwood said woodenly.

'Is my wife there?'

'She went to bed just after the call came through. Would you like to speak to her mother?'

Tarrant said, 'No, I wouldn't.' He hung up and then phoned Harper. He didn't sound any too friendly either.

'I've been expecting you to call,' Harper said.

'I gather you've heard from Drabble?'

'About half an hour ago.'

'And?'

'Well, as you must know, he's got the beacon and the recognition panels. He wants the Wessex helicopter positioned at Wyton, which is near St Ives, and he said that he will phone at 1000 hours to give me the compass heading and the wireless frequency.'

'Is everything set up for him?'

Harper avoided the question. 'When are you coming back?' he said.

'I'm stranded.'

'What?'

'They just made their first big mistake, they stole the Zephyr.'

'Have you informed the police?'

'Not yet, but I will as soon as we finish this call.'

There was a brief silence and then Harper said, 'Unfortunately, the police won't have enough time to trace the car before Drabble calls tomorrow.'

His attitude alarmed Tarrant and he said, 'About the helicopter?'

'What about it?'

'It is okay, isn't it?'

'Of course it is. Everything will be fine so long as the pilot can pick up the signal from the beacon. Call me tomorrow morning after ten, all right?'

Tarrant said he would do that and hung up. It wasn't until he had reported the theft of his car to the police and they were giving him a lift into Leicester, that the significance of Harper's remark about the beacon sank in. The Wessex was going to take off and fly on the course set by Drabble and it was going to keep on flying right over the pick-up point and afterwards the pilot would report that he had failed to hear the beacon. There were not enough words in the gutter to describe the way he felt about Harper.

The height of the Cuban missile crisis had been the last occasion when Harper had found it necessary to sleep the night in his office, and during the intervening years, he had forgotten the narrowness and comparative discomfort of a camp bed. He lay there in the dark cocooned in a nylon sleeping bag, while a too active mind and the sound of thunder in the distance kept him awake.

For all that he had achieved at the end of a long and frustrating day, he could have paid a flying visit to Bisley to watch Vincent and his team going through their paces. There was something very satisfying about seeing a good shot in action, and although most people preferred to watch from the firing point, he liked to stand in the butts listening to the crack of each round passing over his head as it entered the target above. He tried to picture the range in his mind but Drabble kept intruding, and he wondered, not for the first time, why a group of men should have chosen to operate under that name. He recalled Churchill's dictum that any code name allotted to a future operation should not be pessimistic or over-optimistic or indicate the nature and intention of the plan. He believed now that the significance of 'Drabble' lay in the fact that it disclosed absolutely nothing.

The phone trilled sharply in the stillness of the room and he scrambled out of bed to answer it.

A strange voice said, 'Mr Harper?'

'Yes,' he said, 'who's calling?'

'Duty Officer, sir—Section One.'

'Have you got a name?'

'I have,' said the stranger. 'Can we go to secure speech?'

Harper said, 'Wait.' He groped his way around the desk, felt for and found the button on the scrambler. 'All right,' he said, 'go ahead.'

'My name is Illingworth, sir. I've been trying to contact Mr Julyan on a rather urgent matter. I've rung him at home but there was no answer, and so I decided I had better call you.'

'Why?'

'Because I understand you are an old friend, and your wife thought you might know where I could find him.'

'My wife?'

'Yes. I'm afraid I disturbed her for nothing but I thought you would be at home.'

'Normally I am.' Harper was suddenly conscious that he was being unreasonable and he changed his tone of voice. 'I'm sorry,' he said, 'but I don't know what to suggest. Perhaps his phone is out of order?'

'No, sir, the GPO have checked it and the local police tell me they can't get him to answer the door either. It seems the house is empty.'

'The police? How are they involved?'

'I'm afraid they have some distressing news. Mrs Julyan and her son were killed in a traffic accident outside Lyon earlier this evening.'

'Oh God,' Harper said quietly. He tried to put himself in Julyan's place because he knew that such a shocking piece of news would break him completely. 'What happened to the little girl?'

'I understand she has been seriously injured. That's why it's essential I get in touch with Mr Julyan as soon as possible. They want him to fly out there straight away.'

'I see.'

'Yes, I'm afraid it's a bad business all round. There was another man with her—an American smuggler, who was killed outright.'

'What's this about a smuggler?' Harper said quickly.

'He was carrying a large number of uncut diamonds in a money belt.'

'Jesus Christ.'

'Sir?'

Harper said, 'I'll meet you at Julyan's house in twenty minutes.'

'I can't leave the office.'

'You can, and you will, and you'll make sure that the police are there too. Your Mr Julyan is about to defect.'

'I don't believe it.'

'You'd better,' Harper said grimly. He hung up before Illingworth had a chance to question him further.

He experienced a sense of personal betrayal which left a nasty taste in his mouth. If a man like Edward Julyan was not to be trusted, who could he trust? They had been close friends for many years and it had never entered his mind to question Edward's loyalty. A man with a record such as his was beyond doubt. Christ, he'd become a legend in his own lifetime, collecting a DSO and the Croix de Guerre for his work with the French Section during the war, and he had earned those medals twice over for the risks he'd taken in the so-called years of peace.

His hand reached for the telephone. The Minister would be distressed but there would be no quibbling over small details. Although he was now free to handle the situation the way he saw fit, Harper felt there was little cause for satisfaction.

The storm was right overhead now and the rain began to fall, lightly at first but then with increasing severity.

Saturday

SEVENTH DAY

18

THE HOUSE WAS CALLED DOWNDALE AND IT STOOD IN Priory Road opposite the Upper Chine Girls' School, and the curious thing was that he had no recollection of ever having visited it before because he knew that his aunt had sold the place in 1943 when he was still a child, and in those days the Isle of Wight was virtually a prohibited area and visitors from the mainland were discouraged. And yet he was there with Alex in his aunt's house and their bedroom looked out over the sloping lawn and the huge tulip tree blotted out most of the sunlight. And Alex was in white satin and there was a lace veil over her face, and that too was crazy because they had been married in Bradford. And he had stood there with his back to the window and he had watched her remove the veil, and then suddenly it wasn't Alex but her mother who was there in the room with him, and her cold grey eyes behind the rimless glasses seemed to mock him. And then the scene changed and he was walking down to Apley steps towards the crowded beach, and he knew he was supposed to be looking for Alex, and for some obscure reason he asked the candyfloss man on the promenade if he knew where she was, and the man had smiled and said, 'Didn't you know? She's away at a funeral in Lake.' And he had run all the way to the cemetery and he had found her standing alone above the open grave, and he had tried to tell her that it was no one's fault that Sarah had been killed, and then she had looked at him in a strange way and said, 'I'm here because today we are going to bury David.'

He woke up in the dark, and although his body was bathed in sweat, he shivered convulsively as if in the throes of malaria. A sickening feeling that there was little he could do to help his son now gnawed at him and slowly and insidiously sapped his resolution. He thought about Alex and wished that they could face the long day ahead together. He lay there, his arms folded behind his head as he waited for the first light of morning to come shafting into the room and with it, the sounds of a city coming to life. If Alex had been at hand, she would have counselled rest, but he was alone in a hotel bedroom and his unquiet mind posed one complex fantasy after another.

If he was going to foul things up through the helicopter pilot, Harper had to have some plan in mind. The Wessex pilot would have them pinpointed the moment he homed in on the beacon and located the recognition panels marking the landing site, but he wouldn't be able to radio back the information because Drabble would be monitoring that frequency. He couldn't hover over the landing site either, if the excuse for not making the contact was that the beacon was malfunctioning. So he would have to circle the area while reporting over the air that the beacon signal was too weak to pinpoint. Drabble wouldn't answer him because he would be running the risk of having his position fixed by intercept, but every RAF Station within fifty miles could pick up the transmissions from the Wessex and get a radar bearing. Harper would end up with a triangle of error but he would know that his quarry was somewhere in the centre of it.

The question was, would Drabble believe that the beacon was malfunctioning? Bad weather was something which neither party could anticipate, but an unserviceable beacon wasn't in the category of an unexpected hazard. In his own mind, Tarrant felt certain that Drabble would never swallow it.

The first light of day began to filter into the darkened room and Tarrant rolled out of bed, strode over to the windows and drew back the curtains. The weather would not be an ally this day; the thunderstorm had veered away before it had reached the Midlands, and it looked as if it was going to be warm and close again.

So, all right, he thought, Drabble will know that we are lying about the beacon because we want to locate him, but that doesn't mean he will automatically pull the switch on David. If he kills David, he has no bargaining factor left; David is his passport to safety. It was the only comforting thought to hold on to. If it was left to Harper, he would locate the pick-up point, throw a cordon around the area, and then move in, and he might just not have the safety of David paramount in his mind. No matter how futile or illogical, Tarrant knew that he had to do something. He couldn't leave it entirely to chance and Harper.

He turned away from the window and forced himself to do the mundane things of life. He couldn't shave but at least he could wash, since the hotel had thoughtfully provided him with a towel and a minute tablet of soap. No one would mistake him for a tramp, but as he would be wearing a rumpled suit and a shirt which smelt of yesterday's sweat, he would hardly make an impressive figure. Before the day was out, he would have to approach total strangers for help; he hoped his appearance wouldn't put them off. In the long hours before breakfast, he compiled a list of points to check out; if nothing else, it helped to kill time.

The soft light of early morning touched the silver birch trees in the copse and brought the Dutch barn, the stables and the Georgian house into sharp relief. To the casual, untrained eye, Hillglade Farm presented the sort of peaceful and timeless scene which looked well on a calendar, but the random eye could not detect the hidden sentries who kept watch over the empty fields.

Calvert, a dead cigarette clinging to his lower lip, sat on a wooden chair in the kitchen nursing a 30-calibre Springfield carbine in his arms. From where he sat, he had an oblique view of the hall and the back door. Upstairs in the room next to the one occupied by Julyan, Silk was wide awake, a loaded Sten gun within easy reach. Although there was little chance that he could be seen from the road, he sat to one side of the net-curtained window while he observed the narrow, sunken lane which ran past the front of the house and joined the minor road just before the village of Melton Basset. For the very sick, between two and four in the morning is the time of crisis when the human spirit is at its lowest ebb, and it is also during these hours that the risk of a police raid is at its peak. Both Calvert and Silk knew this full well and had made a point of being alert.

Ruth Burroughs was also awake, but for different reasons. The chance encounter with the Scotsons had unnerved her, and although she had convinced Calvert that there was nothing to worry about, a nagging doubt remained in her mind. There was a faint possibility that Tarrant had not been listening to their conversation, but even if he had, of what use was a name to him? She had done nothing which could have aroused his suspicion and he had no reason to connect her with the theft of his car. It was a comfortable hypothesis and she wished she could be convinced of its validity. It had been a mistake not to confide in McKee, but at the time she had thought it best not to, because she was afraid that Paul would really go to pieces if he thought they were in imminent danger. He was already drinking heavily but at least he was sober during the day, and even now, when they were only a few hours away from freedom, it was still necessary to keep up appearances. If any gossip got back to Melton Basset they could be in trouble. The more she thought about it, the more convinced Ruth Burroughs became that McKee had to be told. She satisfied herself that Paul was still fast asleep, and then pushing the bedclothes to one side, she slipped out and tiptoed out of their bedroom.

McKee slept on his stomach, his right hand thrust beneath the pillow was folded around the butt of a Colt ·38 automatic,

while the index finger rested on the trigger guard. The faint
creak as the door was opened brought him out of a light sleep,
and instinctively he rolled out of bed and landed softly facing
the intruder. His thumb flipped the safety catch on to fire and
he held the automatic steady in both hands.

Ruth Burroughs said quietly, 'Are you awake, Andrew?'

He put the catch back to safe and climbed into bed again.
'You want to be more careful,' he said, 'you almost got your head
blown off. What do you want?'

'I've got to talk to you.'

'Yes?'

'About last night.' She came and sat on the edge of his bed.

'Does it have to be now?'

'Yes.'

'What about Paul?'

'He's asleep.'

'I don't want you making any trouble between us,' McKee
whispered savagely.

'I don't propose to.'

'All right, so long as you remember that. Now, what's bother-
ing you?'

'I bumped into the Scotsons at the Cross Keys and they saw
me with Calvert.'

'What happened?' McKee said warily.

'I think I passed it off and they were faintly amused to see me
with another man, but I'm not sure if Tarrant heard my name
or not.'

'There must be thousands of Ruths about.'

She moistened her lips. 'The Scotsons were in a group,' she
whispered hesitantly, 'and I was introduced to the other members of their party as Ruth Burroughs.'

'You and Calvert were supposed to keep an eye on Tarrant
while Silk lifted the Zephyr, right?'

'Yes.'

'Did you speak to him?'

'For a while.'

'But you didn't make it seem obvious?'

'I don't think so.'

'You don't sound very sure?'

'I'm not a mind reader.'

'How did Tarrant react? Did he appear to be suspicious?'

'No.'

'Was he eavesdropping when you were talking to the Scotsons?'

'I don't know.'

'Fucking hell, is there anything you do know? Three years at a university and all you can say is, I don't know. You're supposed to be one of the intelligentsia.'

'I'm not stupid.'

'You could have fooled me,' he snarled. 'Did the expression on his face give anything away?'

'I can't say, I deliberately avoided looking at him too much.'

'You're supposed to be a trained agent. Did he hang around your party?'

'No, he left the bar a few minutes after the Scotsons arrived and played the fruit machines.'

'He took a sudden interest in the gaming machines, did he?'

'Yes. I'm sure he was embarrassed. You know—he felt in the way.' McKee lay silent and she said tentatively, 'Andrew?'

'What?'

'Supposing he checks up on me?'

McKee considered the problem. 'We've still got the boy,' he said, 'he's the ace up our sleeve.'

'Would you kill him?'

'If necessary.'

'They might not believe that.'

'They will. If anything goes wrong and they surround this house, I mean to fight it out.'

She drew in her breath sharply. 'Isn't there an alternative?' she whispered.

'Our people won't make a trade because they have no one to

exchange, and I doubt if they will own us after the way we've been forced to operate.'

'I'm frightened.'

'There's no need to be. Up to now we've been several jumps ahead of them and nothing has happened to change that.'

But it had. Their luck had started to turn, and McKee knew it. In a moment of pessimism, which was totally out of character, he thought about the records clerk whose office was located in the basement of the Lubianka. For him, total failure was simply a matter of taking correct documentary action. He would extract their cards from the index system, and being a very thorough man, he would check to make sure that he had not made a mistake, and perhaps in doing so, he would read those cards with interest. Those postcard-sized bits of paper represented their life histories. Would he spare a thought for:

KALININE, Andrei, Alias Andrew McKee, born Minsk 26 September 1925. Parents: Father—Sergei Kalinine, Commissar with V. I. Kuznetsov's 3rd Army, executed on or about 6 August 1941 by SS Kommando Dietmeir. Mother—Galina Kalinine née Gaponovich, killed 28th June 1941. Record of Service: Colonel KGB. Awarded Order of the Red Star 1943, Medal for Battle Merit 1943, Medal for Valour 1945. Current assignment: Controller Borodino Cell.

Or for:

PILDULSKI, Davina, Alias Ruth Burroughs, born New York 17 June 1940. Parents: Father—'Pan' Pildulski (Polish National), now deceased. Mother—Corinne Humbert (American National), present whereabouts unknown. Parents divorced 22 May 1941. Mother consented to father having custody of child. Father and daughter returned Poland via Mexico City 10 July 1946. Record of Service: Graduate Warsaw University with Arts Degree specialising in languages 1961. Entered KGB service 6 February 1962. Drafted

United Kingdom 4 April 1964. Married ANDERS, Stefan, alias Paul Burroughs, at Lincoln Registry Office 9 April 1965. Current assignment: Cypher Operator Borodino Cell.

Or for:

ANDERS, Stefan, alias Paul Burroughs, born Lvov 2 January 1929. Parents: Father—Bor Anders. Moved family to Soviet Union 11 December 1938 because of persecution of Communists (Note: Bor Anders joined CP in 1924). Lived in Odessa. Father killed in action at Kharkov on or about 22 November 1941. Mother—Ilena Anders, died natural causes Moscow 6 October 1951. Record of Service: degree in Agriculture Moscow University. Entered KGB service 3 March 1951. Drafted United Kingdom 21 September 1962. Married PILDULSKI, Davina, alias Ruth Burroughs, 9 April 1965. Current assignment: Radio Operator Borodino Cell.

The hell he would, thought McKee. That dedicated clerk would feed those three cards into the destructor and he would stand there until they had been sliced into tiny shreds, and he wouldn't give a damn. And he wouldn't know about Calvert and Silk because their records weren't kept in the Lubianka. Only three cards and the Borodino Cell ceased to exist.

In this, McKee was wrong. There was a fourth in respect of Oleg Knoiev, alias Crosby, alias Mark Jarman, alias Marcel Vergat, alias Walter J. Outram; a captain in the KGB whose record included a special commendation for his work with counter-intelligence which had resulted in the Court Martial of five army officers assigned to the GRU Directorate of the Moscow Military District. But of course McKee was not aware that the man he knew as Jarman and Vergat was already dead.

Tarrant had an early breakfast at seven-thirty and read through the *Daily Express* and the *Daily Telegraph* while he ate to see if there was any mention of David. There wasn't, but there was a lot of coverage given to the Australian Touring Team, England's hopefuls in the Munich Olympics and the Nations' Cup. The world of sport, however, held little interest for him at that moment in time.

Fifteen minutes later he left the dining-room and checked with the police to see if they had any news of the Zephyr and learned that they were still looking for it. They appeared to think that it might have been taken for a joyride and they seemed confident that they would recover it before the day was out. Tarrant didn't share their optimism, but he thanked them politely and then, looking up Hertz in the Yellow Pages, called to ask if they could deliver a self-drive car to the hotel.

They offered him a Volkswagen at £3.95 a day with one hundred miles free motoring, after which it would cost him two pence a mile plus the petrol. He could either top the car up with petrol himself or they would do it for him at the end of the hire period and deduct the cost from the £10 deposit. They also operated a collision damage waiver of sixty-five pence and a personal accident cover costing another twenty-five pence. Tarrant said he was prepared to accept their offer.

He looked through the telephone directory to see what they had listed under Army. As far as Leicestershire was concerned, it was pretty thin on the ground. There was a Veterinary Corps Depot at Melton Mowbray, a Pay Office in South Wigston and a Careers Information Office in Charles Street. He made a note of their address and decided to call on them first.

He paid his hotel bill, took delivery of the Volkswagen, and then asked the way to Charles Street. Finding the Office wasn't difficult, finding a place to park was a different matter. He ended up a mile from the Careers and Information Office and walked back.

The sergeant manning the reception desk seemed a little disappointed when Tarrant produced his ID card dispelling any illusion that he might be an applicant. He asked for, and got, the performance data on the Wessex and a set of quarter-inch maps covering England and Wales. They also gave him the use of one of their interview rooms on the second floor where he set about joining the maps together. At the back of Tarrant's mind there was a vague idea that he might be able to fix Drabble's position by dead reckoning once he knew the compass heading of the Wessex.

19

THE USUAL STEPS HAD BEEN TAKEN, AND FOR ONCE, Harper was satisfied that the close watch on ports of embarkation and airfields, which had been effectively established by 0500 hours, was not a case of shutting the stable door after the horse had bolted. He was absolutely certain that Julyan was still in England and he meant to have him. He was not clear in his own mind yet exactly how this was to be achieved, but he was confident that once he had located their hide-out through the Sarbe beacon, it would not be difficult to cordon it off, but thereafter he would have to tackle the problem as the situation developed.

Ideally, he wanted to incapacitate the opposition before they moved in, but much would depend on the sort of place that Drabble had chosen to use as a hide. He had, in any event, already decided against CS gas, for he considered it likely that they had equipped themselves with respirators, and tear smoke was hardly a surprise weapon—it gave ample warning of its presence and they would know immediately that they were under attack. Psychochemicals were the answer, since they were odourless, tasteless and invisible, and it was just possible that he might be able to contaminate their water supply with LSD. This drug would induce a confused state of mind and impair physical performance, but it also had undesirable side effects; it could release all inhibitions and radically change a pattern of behaviour, and once self-control had vanished, anyone under the influence of this drug became unpredictable. If threatened with conventional force, Drabble might or might not kill David, but if he became irrational he wouldn't hesitate to do so.

Harper pulled over to the kerb and stopped the car outside the flat. With any luck this would be his last visit, and from a personal viewpoint, he would not be sorry to see the last of Tarrant and his family. He had shown them too much sympathy and that had been an error, for now, looking back over the past week, he knew he would have handled things differently if Mulholland had not persuaded him to see Tarrant. He told himself that he would have taken a much firmer line with Drabble from the outset. He walked up the steps and rang the bell and presently Alex answered the door.

Some of the strain of the last few days had slipped away and she was less brittle. She was, Harper thought, a very attractive woman and she had taken some trouble with her appearance, and this in itself was a sign of hope. He followed her into the lounge and was relieved to see that her mother was not present. He did not greatly care for that lady, and was inclined to think that she wielded too much influence over her daughter.

Alex said quietly, 'I know it's foolish, but I have a feeling that this nightmare will soon be over.'

'It's not foolish to hope,' he said.

The reply seemed to disconcert her. 'When do you think we will get David back?' she said anxiously.

Harper disliked being pinned down, but he couldn't ignore her question. 'Monday or Tuesday, all being well.' He realised that he had said too much and corrected himself hastily, 'I'm not too sure of the BOAC schedules,' he said coolly, 'they may not have a flight from Brazil.'

'But couldn't David return with the VC 10?'

'Yes, he could, but the RAF are not carrying a slip crew on this trip. They would need to rest before the return flight.'

She played nervously with the rings on the third finger of her left hand. 'I see,' she said faintly. 'Would you like a cup of coffee?'

Harper smiled. 'I hardly think we have time for one, do you?' The phone started to ring urgently. 'There you are,' he said calmly, 'I expect that will be Drabble.'

The green-coloured Austin Mini turned off the minor road into the narrow, sunken lane which led up to Hillglade Farm. Hidden from view by the tall hedgerows on either side of the track, the Mini crawled on for the better part of half a mile and then swung sharp left into the yard and stopped outside the kitchen. McKee got out of the car and stretched his arms above his head. His eyes took in the Dutch barn, the stables, the copse which screened the eastern side of the house, and the open fields beyond the neat post-and-rail fence at the far end of the yard, and nothing seemed unusual, but then, as he was so completely in control of the situation, McKee had little reason to suppose that anything would go wrong. The Alsatian lying in the shade of the stables chose that moment to start barking. McKee picked up a stone and hurled it at the dog and the barking ended in a yelp of pain. He turned away and walked into the house where the others were waiting for him.

As soon as he entered the lounge he could see from the expressions on their faces that they were keyed up.

'You can relax,' he said. 'Harper won't give us any trouble, he's practically eating out of my hand.'

'That doesn't sound like the man I know,' said Julyan.

'Then you don't know him very well, and he doesn't know you either, does he, friend?' McKee said icily. 'I bet he never thought of you as just a grubby little man who could be bought by the highest bidder.'

'We have a business deal.'

'That we have.'

'I'm merely telling you not to underestimate him.'

'I don't intend to, because from this moment we are going to turn the farm into a strongpoint and everyone, including you, will carry a gun. Silk will cover the lane outside the front of the house from the landing and Calvert will stand guard over the boy in the end room upstairs.' He looked at Julyan. 'And you, friend,' he said, 'will stay in the kitchen and watch the back. Ruth will be in the dining-room across the hall from you, and I will be monitoring the helicopter waveband in case Harper tries anything.' He paused, glanced round the assembled group and said, 'Any questions so far?'

Burroughs said, 'Where do you want the radio?'

'In my room. As soon as you have set it up, I'll tell you when and where to put out the recognition panels and the beacon, and when that has been done, you'll come back to the house and stay in this room. Got it?'

Burroughs said, 'You make it sound simple enough.'

'It will be, if you all do as you're told.'

'About the boy?' said Calvert.

'I'm coming to him,' said McKee. 'He stays in the cellar until 1230 and then we'll rig the harness on him and take him upstairs. I'll need your help to do that.'

'What's the plan for getting into the helicopter?' said Julyan.

'We wait until it touches down on the pad, then I go out first with the boy, followed by Silk, you, Paul, Ruth and Calvert in that order.' He waited briefly to see if there were any other questions, and then he said, 'All right, let's get started.'

Time was working against Tarrant, and yet he was forced to squander it until it was safe to assume that Drabble had been in touch. He waited until ten past ten and then he rang through. Alex answered the phone.

Tarrant said, 'Don't worry, it's only me. Where's Harper?'

'He just left.'

'Did he say where he was going?'

'He mentioned something about going into the office, but I'm not sure whether that was just for my benefit.' There was a note of suppressed anxiety in her voice that alarmed him.

'What's the matter?' he said.

'I'm not sure. I have a feeling that Mr Harper was keeping something from me.'

'Oh, why?'

'It was nothing he said, but he seemed distant and withdrawn, and it was almost as if at the last moment he had decided to abandon David.'

She was close to tears and he sensed that if he was too sympathetic it would only make her feel worse.

'You're imagining things,' he said firmly.

'I hope so, oh God, how I hope so.'

More than anything else, he had to know what Drabble had said, and somehow the conversation had to be led round to that subject without alarming Alex. Tarrant struggled to find the right words, but they wouldn't come, and his silence betrayed him.

Alex said, 'Are you all right, John?'

'I'm fine—just a little tired, that's all. It won't be long now.'

'So Mr Harper said.'

'Oh, when was that?'

'After Drabble spoke to him on the phone.'

It was going to be easier than he had dared hope. 'Let's hear what he had to say for himself,' he said casually.

'What?'

'Play the tape back.'

'I can't, Mr Harper took it away with him.'

'Can you remember what was said?'

'Does it matter now?' she said wearily.

'Please,' he said, 'I'd like to know.'

'He mentioned a compass bearing of 320 degrees. I'm sure of that because he repeated it.'

'Grid or magnetic?'

'Oh God, I don't know. Grid, I think—yes, I'm sure he said grid.'

'That would be logical. Drabble would measure it off the map and leave us to do the conversion.'

'I don't understand . . .'

'Listen,' he said urgently, 'what else was said?'

'Something about wireless frequencies, but I'm afraid I didn't take much notice of that part of the conversation.' Her voice was shaky. 'Why are you questioning me like this?'

He had bungled it, and now that she was on the edge of panic, the questioning would have to stop. 'I'm sorry,' he said quietly, 'I didn't mean to frighten you. I'm just anxious to know what arrangements have been made.' He licked his dry lips. 'You know how much David means to me.'

'Yes,' she said dully, 'he's everything to me too.'

'We'll get him back.'

'Do you really believe we will?'

'I'm certain of it.'

There was a longish pause while each groped for an ending, and then Alex said quickly, 'Come home, John.'

'What?'

'Now. I need you. I can't see this thing through alone.'

'Your mother hasn't left you, has she?' he said incredulously.

'No. But it's you I want.'

It was a long time since she had expressed a need for him, and he felt moved. 'I love you,' he said softly.

'I love you too.' There was a catch in her voice. 'Please come home.'

'I will.'

'When?'

'By the first available train.' It was a lie but a permissible one.

Tarrant replaced the phone, dried his sweating hands on his handkerchief, and then, taking a protractor, marked off 320 degrees from Wyton and projected a line across the map to the point of no return for the Wessex. He was working on an operating range of three hundred miles, and with a sickening feeling, he came to realise that the Wessex could reach a point north of Manchester and still have enough fuel and time in hand to get back to Lyneham where the VC 10 was waiting. He checked the data the RAF had given him, saw that the transmitting range of the Sarbe beacon was in excess of ten miles, and calculated that the pick-up point could be anywhere inside an area measuring fifteen hundred square miles. He had five and a half hours to find Drabble; dead reckoning wasn't the way to do it.

He told himself that no one was perfect, and Drabble was no exception, and that if he really thought about it, there must be something that had been overlooked. He went back to the map, located the Cross Keys and studied the surrounding area. A car didn't simply disappear into thin air, and the Zephyr must have been a millstone around their necks from the moment they had stolen it. The thief had no way of knowing when its loss would be reported, but in the circumstances, they might have counted on thirty minutes before the alarm was given, and a good driver could make thirty miles in that space of time. On the map scale, thirty miles worked out at seven and a half inches, and a circle of that radius, centred on the Cross Keys, took in Mansfield, Stamford, Northampton, Coventry and Burton on Trent, and that was still a big area to search. It was some time before Tarrant remembered that Drabble's first telephone call had been traced to somewhere in Northampton.

Even a helicopter as large as a Wessex could land almost anywhere, but they had asked for a beacon and a set of recognition panels, and they were hardly likely to put those to use in the middle of a built-up area. In their shoes, Tarrant thought he would opt for a landing site well away from any town or village but very close to the place where David was held captive. It seemed to him that an isolated farm was a fair bet.

There were a number of such farms within the circle he had drawn on the map, and he was going to need all the help he could get if the choice was to be narrowed down. He asked the staff of the Careers Office for the name of the biggest Estate Agent in the area, and they told him that Platt, Swaffen and Mace had branches all over the East Midlands. He didn't have far to go; their main office was just across the street.

The girl, who introduced herself as Miss Peters, was very polite but equally she seemed resolved to keep Tarrant at arm's length, and he regretted not having borrowed a razor. It appeared that Platt and Swaffen were deceased and that Mr Mace was not available, but she suggested that perhaps she might be able to help him.

Tarrant said, 'Perhaps you can.' He produced his ID card and held it just far enough away so that she was unable to see the details clearly. 'I'm making an official enquiry.'

'I'm sorry,' she said quickly, 'I didn't realise you were from the police. Perhaps you'd like to see Mr Eric?'

'Who's he?'

'He manages this office for his uncle, Mr Mace. Who shall I say is calling?'

'Tarrant.'

She smiled quickly. 'Please excuse me,' she said, 'I won't keep you a minute.'

She disappeared into an inner room and he caught a low murmur of voices, and then presently she came back and said, 'Mr Eric will see you now.'

Mr Eric was not yet thirty and his taste in clothes stopped just short of being trendy. His brown hair rested on the shoulders of a well-cut jacket which had been tailored with a lean figure in mind, and it was obvious from the look on her face that Miss Peters found him attractive. Somehow, Tarrant was not altogether surprised to find that he had a limp handshake.

'What can I do for you, Superintendent?' he said.

'I'm afraid your secretary is mistaken. I'm a Major in the army.'

He raised his eyebrows. 'I wonder how I got the impression you were a police officer?' he said acidly. He wasn't very tall, and like a good many small men, he could be pompous and over-bearing.

Tarrant said, 'I don't suppose my name rings a bell with you?'

'No. Should it?'

'On Sunday last, two boys were abducted. One of them, a boy called James Stroud, was found near Barnard Castle on Monday morning; the other, my son, is still missing.'

A frown creased his narrow forehead. 'Now you mention it,' he said, 'I do remember seeing a small paragraph about it.'

'I think you might be able to help me.'

'In what way?'

'My son is being held in an isolated farm somewhere within a radius of thirty miles of this city. The farm I have in mind could have a paddock, but on the other hand it might even be a small-holding, but it will certainly be some distance from the nearest habitation. I'd like you to go through your records and find me some likely addresses.'

'That's rather a tall order.'

'I realise that,' Tarrant said wearily.

'I don't think you quite understand. A lot would depend on when this farm changed hands. How far back do we search? Six months? A year? Two years? or what?'

'I don't know, it could be much longer than that.'

'Quite honestly, Major Tarrant, I think you're wasting your time. Why not leave this matter to the police?'

'Would you, in my position?'

'I can't give you an honest answer to that one, I'm not married.' He pursed his lips. 'I want to help you,' he said, 'if you'd like to call back later this afternoon, say round about four o'clock, I might have something for you.'

'Time is one thing I haven't got,' said Tarrant. 'It's now five minutes to eleven; let's see what you can get me in the next hour.'

'We'll barely scratch the surface in an hour, but if you care to wait in Miss Peters' office, I'll get in touch with our other branches and see what we can do.'

He sat on a bench seat facing a wall covered with colour photographs of other people's houses, most of which had already been sold. The girl pecked at the typewriter and answered the phone whenever it rang, but Tarrant noticed that her attention was directed at the clock above his head, and he thought that, unlike him, she was probably wishing the time away.

Between Drabble and Harper, he felt as if he was being crushed in a vice. He was reluctantly being driven to the conclusion that, for all the good he was doing, he might just as well be at home with Alex. At least he might be of some practical use there, instead of which he was waiting on a forlorn hope that Platt, Swaffen and Mace might just turn up something.

Wasn't it stupid to go on hoping when Drabble had demonstrated time and again that he was the complete professional? He hadn't put a foot wrong except perhaps when it came to stealing the Zephyr, and there luck had been with him. Or had it? A man who planned each move with such infinite care would never chance his arm at the final and most crucial stage. At any time, Tarrant could have walked outside and caught them breaking into his car and Drabble must surely have thought of that possibility and taken steps to prevent it happening? And Jesus, Drabble had. He had planted someone inside the Cross Keys to keep him occupied, and that someone was either Calvert, Scotson or Burroughs, or was it Burrows? He began to wonder if any of them happened to live on a farm.

Tarrant said, 'Miss Peters?'

'Yes?'

'Have you a telephone directory?'

'Yes, of course; which one would you like?—Leicester, Derby, Lincoln, Nottingham or Northamptonshire?'

'The lot,' he said.

Ten minutes later he found what he was looking for: Burroughs, P., Hillglade Farm, Hillglade Lane, near Melton Basset.

20

THE LONG HOURS OF CONFINEMENT IN THE DARK CELLAR had left their mark upon the boy. His face was like wax, and where he had wet himself, the smell of urine was strong. He had tried desperately hard to control his bladder, hoping that the woman would let him go to the lavatory when she came with his breakfast on a tray, but this morning he had not been fed, and finally he could hold it no longer, and close to tears, he had allowed his body to function. The urine passing through his penis had felt as if it was scalding him but it was nothing to the burning sense of shame he now felt.

McKee said, 'You're going to stink the plane out, sonny. I can see that we shall have to sit you near the tail where we shan't be able to smell you.' He could read the fear in the boy's eyes and he was well satisfied. He knew the true purpose of terror and he subscribed to Lenin's view that people who were frightened usually did as they were told. He removed the gag, untied him and dragged the boy off the bed.

Calvert said, 'He doesn't look too steady on his feet to me.'

'Neither would you,' said McKee, 'if you'd been through what he has.' He looked at David and smiled bleakly. 'I expect you've got pins and needles,' he said. 'We shall have to restore your circulation, won't we? Suppose you start running on the spot.'

There was a moment of hesitation and McKee smacked his

face. It was not a hard blow but it was enough to show that he expected to be obeyed. The exercise period lasted for ten minutes and by the time it was over, David's face was brick red, his hair was dark with sweat and his chest was heaving.

McKee gave him a few minutes to catch his breath before they rigged the harness around his stomach and shoulders. The three silver bells at the waist should have been a reminder of innocent childhood, but instead they lent the final obscene touch to the macabre set of reins. They were a tight fit, and the leather straps bit into and bruised his skin.

McKee said, 'We've been feeding you too well.'

David licked his lips and then nervously, he said, 'The lady didn't bring me anything to eat this morning.'

'It's just as well she didn't, otherwise we'd never have got you into this harness.'

He cast a professional eye over the fourteen canvas pouches which between them contained seven pounds of plastic explosive and satisfied himself that the firing circuit would not malfunction. He picked up the length of cable which had been attached to the push–pull switch and waved it under David's nose.

'You see this,' McKee said harshly, 'it's your tail; step on it accidentally and there will be nothing left of you.'

Little now remained to be done. They would pinion the boy's arms and gag him and then he would be led upstairs and placed in the end room where he would be guarded by Calvert. McKee would be like a commander watching over the battlefield from an observation post and he needed his hostage to be close at hand in case anything did go wrong at the very last minute.

They were a stick of eight, and they had practised getting in and out of the Wessex helicopter until their leader was satisfied that their timing could not be bettered. They struck the aircrew as being an oddly assorted bunch, for they wore no recognisable uniform and yet each man was armed, and it was evident that they were a tightly knit and highly disciplined group of men. Their ages ranged from the early twenties to the mid-forties, and a few of their number spoke with marked foreign accents. The pilot, inclined to think that some of them were refugees from Eastern Europe, had mentioned this to Harper in jocular fashion, and had regretted it ever since.

Harper, deep in thought, stood apart from the others. A top official who was determined to cross over was always a difficult man to detect before the event. Edward Julyan was not a low-grade clerk or junior officer who was obliged to photograph secretly the information he proposed to sell; he carried everything in his head like a walking computer. He had no need to send for files which he was not authorised to see; everything concerning Eastern Europe automatically came to him and all he had had to do was to memorise the details. After his defection was made known, any number of people would say that of course the security services were slipping because it must have been perfectly obvious to anyone that Julyan had been living above his means. These same people, he thought bitterly, would raise a shrill scream of protest if their own private lives were put under a microscope in the interests of security. In a democracy, you have to respect the rights of the individual and accept a degree of risk or else you were fast on the road to becoming a police state.

He wondered if Drabble had already persuaded Julyan that, as an act of good faith, he should part with some of the information he had stored away in his mind. Harper was familiar with the technique of ultra-high-speed transmissions and he knew that the chance of intercepting and jamming any message sent to Moscow by this means was remote. As far as the SIS were concerned, this would really put the cat in amongst the pigeons, but on balance, he thought it unlikely that Julyan would deliver anything until he laid his hands on the diamonds.

He was personally satisfied that he had taken appropriate steps to see that Drew and Vincent and their teams were suitably equipped, but he wished to avoid the use of force if possible. He had a strong feeling that he was up against a number of highly trained KGB operatives, and a lot of useful information was there for the asking if he could take them alive. He planned to isolate the hide and then talk them into surrendering, and he had taken steps to prepare the ground for this. At half-hourly intervals starting at 1330 hours, the BBC news bulletin would contain a reference to the tragic death of Mrs Melissa Julyan. A wolfish smile appeared on Harper's face; Drabble and his friends might think it was a lie, but they couldn't be sure, and he could imagine what it would do to Julyan, and that in turn was bound to have an effect on the others.

He checked the time, and then signalling to Drew and Vincent to get their men on board the waiting helicopter, he walked over to have one last word with the pilot and navigator. He said, 'I want to make one thing absolutely clear—a boy's life is at risk, and if we make a mistake, he will be the one to pay for it. The whole object of this mission is to pinpoint the target, and there is every chance that the enemy will be monitoring our frequency and may—and I only say may—contact us by voice. As soon as we are riding on the beacon and you have sighted the recognition panels, I want you to come up with a May Day call and make a forced landing away from the pick-up point. If possible, I would like you to select a place which is in dead ground. Can you do that and make it appear convincing?'

The pilot said, 'I think so. I'll report a power failure as we veer away from the target and shut off one of the engines. We'll come down with a bump but we should get away with it.'

'I hope you're a good actor.'

'Don't worry about that, I'll be scared enough to convince anyone.'

Harper looked at his wrist-watch again. 'I think we ought to make a move,' he said.

He followed the crewman into the passenger compartment, sat down in one of the canvas seats to the right of the door and fastened his seat belt. A few seconds later, the turbines whined into life, the rotor blades thrashed the air above his head and the Wessex shuddered briefly and then lifted off. The landscape flashed by beneath them.

For a brief moment he envied Wray, even if he was off on a wild-goose chase. A weekend in Luxembourg had its compensations.

The map indicated that Hillglade Farm lay in undulating ground, shielded by a copse on one side and with only a narrow lane affording access to it. Tarrant pulled over on to the grass verge bordering the minor road and stopped just short of the milestone which said Melton Basset—1½ miles. He had no clear idea of what he proposed to do except that there was a vague notion that somehow, if he could get close enough to the man, he would try to talk Drabble into releasing David, and failing that, providing the opportunity arose, he would kill him.

He locked the Volkswagen, and jumping a small ditch, entered the copse. He moved warily, like a cat, keeping to the shadows and pausing frequently to watch and listen, but apart from the occasional car moving along the road behind him, the wood was quiet and still under the hot sun. The trees gradually thinned out and finally stopped just short of a post-and-rail fence some fifteen yards to his front.

The house was Georgian in style, and judging by the number of windows upstairs, he estimated that there were four or five bedrooms. To the left of a solid-looking door there was, in keeping with the character of the house, an imposing mullioned window, while on the right, partially visible behind the green Mini-Cooper parked outside, there was a large expanse of plain glass which he thought might be the kitchen. Some ten to fifteen yards beyond the post-and-rail fence, a Dutch barn obscured most of the stable block on the far side of the yard. The property appeared to be well cared for and expensive, and nothing he had seen so far indicated that this was the place he was looking for. Wanting to get a different view of the house, he decided that he would check out the stables, and since he did not wish to be seen, there was only one way to approach it. He backed into the copse and moved to his left.

The wood narrowed to become a thin belt and then finally it

petered out just beyond the post-and-rail fence at the bottom of the yard where there was a shallow ditch. Nettles grew on either bank amongst the tall grass but the bottom of the ditch was dry and stony. He lowered himself into it and started crawling on his belly. The earth was hard and unyielding and the sweat stung his eyes and ran down his cheeks in rivulets. Somewhere off to his right, a dog barked excitedly, and then he could hear it running about in the yard, and he assumed that it had just been let out of the house. High above his head, a Vulcan bomber from RAF Waddington left white vapour trails in the blue sky.

It was slow, grinding work and the nettles raised white lumps on his hands and face, and his heart was thumping against his ribs. He covered nearly thirty yards and then, satisfied that he was opposite the stable block, he ventured to poke his head above the ditch. The yard was deserted except for the Alsatian which lay facing the house in the shade of the Dutch barn. From his position, Tarrant could see that the stables were oblong in shape, and in line with the gate at the far end of the fence, there was a side door which was ajar. He stepped up out of the ditch, vaulted the fence and ran. The dog, turning its head, caught a fleeting glimpse of him as he disappeared into the stables and started barking.

Tarrant slammed the door behind him and paused long enough to let his eyes get accustomed to the gloom. A horse snorted, another moved restlessly in its stall, but he was hardly aware of them, for beyond the row of stalls in a large open space surrounded by bales of straw, he saw his Zephyr. It was facing a set of double doors and it looked more than a little worse for wear. He supposed that the offside window had been smashed when they pinched the car, and the boot, which had been locked, had obviously been sprung open with a crowbar. He opened the offside door, leaned across the seats and checked the glove compartment, but as he had half-expected, the Browning 9-mm automatic was no longer there. The dog pawing at the door worried him and he looked round for a suitable weapon. He found one in a rusty pitchfork.

Julyan sat in the kitchen listening to the transistor radio. He was no fan of pop music but this was the one occasion when he could not bear to sit in a silent room. The music faded to give way to the news bulletin and it suddenly came home to him that this could well be the last time he would listen to the BBC except for its overseas service. He wondered idly if they broadcast the news in English to Brazil, but even if they didn't, it was a small price to pay for half a million pounds.

And then the bottom fell out of his world as, in a daze, he heard the item which Harper had planted.

The impersonal voice on the radio said, 'Mrs Melissa Julyan, wife of Resistance hero, Colonel Edward Julyan, was killed yesterday evening in a traffic accident near Lyon in France. Mrs Julyan, who was on holiday with her two children...' His hand reached out and switched off the radio, and then his body started to shake and he began to moan. In utter despair, he flung the rifle away and buried his head on his arms. His cry of grief reached their ears and Ruth, McKee and Burroughs came running.

As they entered the room, he looked up and pounded the table with a clenched fist. 'My wife is dead,' he screamed, 'you hear me? Melissa is dead.' The tears coursed down his cheeks. 'Oh, Christ above, what am I to do?'

McKee glanced at the silent transistor. 'The radio,' he shouted, 'you heard it on the radio.' He hit Julyan across the face. 'It was a trick. Get that into your head—it was just a lousy trick of Harper's.'

'But it was on the news,' Julyan said dully, as if there was no disputing its veracity.

'Do you suppose it could be true?' Burroughs said anxiously. His face was the colour of chalk and his voice was unsteady.

Fear was beginning to take hold of everyone except McKee. 'You fucking idiot,' he snarled, 'if you haven't got anything better to do, get out into the yard and shut that bloody dog up.' He caught his breath, and then in a calmer voice said, 'Take the beacon and the panels with you; it's about time they were in position.' He spared a glance for Ruth. 'You look after our friend,' he said, 'I'm wanted upstairs.'

Tarrant could see the man through the crack between the doors. He was tall, thin and balding and he carried a roll of canvas under one arm and the Sarbe beacon in his left hand. He stopped opposite the stables, placed the load on the ground and then walked towards the dog, who was now whining and scratching at the double doors. His suspicions aroused, he slipped his right hand into his pocket and when he took it out again there was a Colt automatic in it. Instinctively, Tarrant backed away into a corner and crouched down behind the bales of straw. He heard the man fumbling with the latch and then both doors swung open and in that instant, he knew he was irrevocably committed to but one course of action.

Tarrant came out of his hiding-place holding the pitchfork as if it were a rifle and bayonet. He was moving fast and when the twelve-inch prongs went into the chest and stomach of the thin, balding man, there was a thrust of one hundred and ninety pounds behind them. The impact lifted the older man off his feet, and as the blood gushed out of his open mouth, he hung there on the end of the fork until his dead weight, acting as a counter balance, brought Tarrant down. They hit the floor together and the sudden jolt broke the shaft of the pitchfork in two.

The Alsatian flew at the tangle of legs on the floor, and as Tarrant rolled to one side and jerked his right leg out of the way, the flashing jaws ripped his trouser leg to shreds. The dog came in for a second try and Tarrant kicked out and caught him flush on the muzzle. It gave him just enough time to come up into the crouch with his left arm extended and bent at the elbow to guard his face. The dog sank its teeth into his forearm, and the blood seeping through the cloth sent it into a frenzy. As it moved its jaws to find a fresh hold, Tarrant hit it between the eyes. Stunned by the blow, the dog backed off shaking its head, and Tarrant swooping, picked up the ·38 Colt automatic, turned and emptied three rounds into the dog as it sprang for his throat. The first bullet shattered a leg, the second hit it in the chest and the third entered its mouth. Carried forward by its own momentum, the dog hit Tarrant in the chest, knocked him back a pace and then fell dead at his feet.

The open yard was a death trap and he knew they would kill him before he was halfway across it unless he used the Zephyr. He scrambled in behind the wheel and his anxious fingers fumbled with the ignition key until at last they found the switch and fired the engine into life. Shifting into first gear, he slipped the handbrake, raced the engine and then let the clutch in fast. The wheels spun, found purchase and then the Zephyr came out of the stables like a bullet. Swinging through a right-angle turn, he pointed it at the house, grated up into second and pushed down on the accelerator until it was flattened out. The engine snarled angrily.

Calvert had retreated into a dream world. Curled up in an armchair, a cigarette hanging from the corner of his mouth, he watched the boy through half-closed eyes while his thoughts wandered elsewhere. More than anything else he wanted to believe McKee, but he couldn't shake off a feeling that the tide was now running against them. He had no idea why the stranger had cracked up but he sensed that some item of bad news had been the cause of it. He knew that if things went really sour, he was expected to fight it out to the end, and the end was death, and he had no wish to die. He thought about the girl he had met last summer in Villefranche, and in a mood of defeatism, wished that he could see her once again. He recalled that her body was soft and brown, and although there was nothing beautiful about the ·30-calibre Springfield carbine which rested on his lap, his right hand caressed the exposed barrel from foresight to breech as lovingly as if it was the body of a woman in heat.

The sound of gunfire and then the noise of the approaching car jerked him sharply back to reality. He leapt to his feet, ran to the window and smashed a pane of glass. Whipping the car-

bine up into his shoulder, he thumbed off the safety and
squeezed off one shot after another. His aim was wild and
erratic, and realising that he had failed to hit the driver, he ran
to the bedroom door and locked it.

A bullet whunked into the bonnet, a second pierced the roof
behind his head and a third clipped the tail and then the car
smashed into the door. The windscreen became a huge spider's
web as a million fine lines traced a crazy pattern across the zone
toughened glass. The bonnet sprang upon and reared up like a
shying horse, and the coolant spewed out of the shattered
radiator, but Tarrant saw none of this. At the moment of impact, he threw the door open and rolled out of the car. He
landed on his left shoulder, went into a forward somersault
and ended up on his hands and knees, and miraculously he
was still holding the automatic. The door, wrenched off its
hinges, was hanging drunkenly askew, and scrambling to his
feet, Tarrant hurled himself through the narrow gap into the
hall.

Ruth was waiting for him, and in her eagerness to be sure of
hitting him, she dwelt too long in the aim and he got in with
three shots while the index finger of her right hand was still
taking up the first pressure on the trigger. Only one found its
mark but it was more than enough. Catching her in the chest, it
knocked Ruth over and she lay there on her back, her heels
drumming on the floor while she stared up at the fast-with-
drawing ceiling, and then the sight left her eyes and the nervous
tattoo stopped.

Julyan, coming out of a state of shock, looked round the
kitchen as if seeing it for the first time, and still in a daze,
noticed that the Lee Enfield rifle was lying on the floor near the
sink unit. The brain knew what had to be done, but he could not
move fast enough. His limbs felt as though he had just got out
of bed for the first time in months, and he lurched across the
room like a drunk. He heard the door burst open and turning in
that direction, he saw Tarrant framed in the entrance, and the
Colt ·38 in his hands was like an accusing finger pointed at his

head. He bent down, his right arm stretching forward to claim the rifle and suddenly he found that it was not within his reach, and because he knew then that he never would be able to make one foot move in front of the other, he waited for death and almost welcomed it. He felt something punch him on the side of the jaw, and for one wild, brief millisecond, his face seemed to be expanding until he was quite sure that it was bigger than a medicine ball, and then everything broke apart.

Tarrant had seen the dead man before, but his mind jibbed, and it was some moments before he connected him with the Intelligence Committee, and then the whole thing became clear. But he had no time to ponder about it for, now that the magazine was empty, the Colt ·38 automatic was just a useless piece of junk. Stepping across Julyan's body, Tarrant, now reduced to being a battlefield scavenger, picked up the Number 5 Lee Enfield rifle. The old habits acquired in training die hard; he opened the bolt a fraction, saw that there was a ·303 round in the breach, and then closed it again. Still not satisfied, he removed the magazine, angled it to the light and counted the number of rounds. He had ten to play with; ten to take him through the rest of the house, and he doubted if it was enough.

He crossed the hall, went into the dining-room and saw the stairs leading to the rooms above where, unknown to him, Silk and McKee waited in ambush on the landing. Cautiously, he edged his way forward and placed one foot on the bottom step of the L-shaped staircase. A sten gun chattered briefly and a few inches above his head, slivers of wood and bits of plaster were gouged out of the wall and the banister rail. An automatic pistol added to the cacophony of noise and the ricochets buzzed like angry bees about him and he jumped back into the dining room and took cover behind the dividing wall.

In the ensuing lull, his ears picked up the distant sound of a helicopter.

McKee shouted, 'You down there, do you hear that? We're home and dry. Nothing can stop us now.'

Tarrant swallowed hard and then found his voice. 'You're

wrong,' he yelled, 'we've both lost—Julyan is dead and they won't make a deal with you.'

'I've still got your son, Tarrant. Either Harper backs off or I kill him. You tell him that.'

'You tell him, he wouldn't believe me.'

Tarrant edged round the wall, pointed the rifle upwards and fired once. The Sten coughed in reply and then stopped abruptly. Costing just thirty shillings when it was first produced early in World War II, the Sten gun was the cheapest machine carbine ever to have been manufactured. Simply designed but crudely finished, it was an effective weapon if the ammunition was loaded into the magazine correctly, otherwise it was prone to jamming. Silk had failed to ensure that all the rounds were seated rim on rim, and as the heavy breech block slammed forward it failed to take the seventh round cleanly into the chamber. Tarrant, hearing the dull clunk, realised that the firer had a stoppage in the breech and made a dash for the stairs. He took them two at a time and fired one round blindly from the hip as he came on.

Silk knew the immediate action drill backwards, and it was simple enough; the firer was required to recock, cant the Sten to the right and shake out the damaged round which was obstructing the breech. He carried this out with the sort of textbook perfection which would have gladdened the heart of any weapon training instructor, but it was just his bad luck that, by the time he was ready to fire, he was in full view of Tarrant who had turned the corner of the L-shaped staircase.

The blood, oozing from the wound in his arm where the dog had bitten him, had made the palm of his left hand slippery and Tarrant found it difficult to keep a firm grip on the rifle. He pulled the butt up into his shoulder but there was no time to take a deliberate aim. He fired rapidly, shotgun style with both eyes open, his right hand opening and closing the bolt and squeezing the trigger in one single co-ordinated motion, and the rifle bucked and the boom of each round mingled with the next to produce a thundering drumbeat.

Silk was hit repeatedly and his body jerked and danced like an animated puppet as both legs, abdominal cavity and chest were rent apart. The Contractor had never been one to pay much attention to the Geneva Convention, and one round of ammunition was pretty much like another as far as he was concerned. The fact that someone at some time in the past had gone to the trouble of flattening out the needle head on each bullet had passed unnoticed. The entry wounds were small but where the dumdum rounds exited, the holes they left were as big as a saucer.

The man swayed above him and then, like a tree felled with an axe, he toppled over and pitched head first towards him, arms and legs flapping like a scarecrow caught in a strong wind, until he came to rest at Tarrant's feet. Sensing that the other man was probably above and behind him, Tarrant swivelled round and fired twice in quick succession.

McKee backed away towards the room where Calvert was guarding the boy, and the Browning in his hand jumped repeatedly as he now pumped one shot after another to keep Tarrant pinned down. He reached behind his back, and trying the door with his free hand, was surprised to find that it was locked.

He kicked his heel against it. 'You stupid bastard,' he shouted, 'unlock this bloody door and bring out the boy.'

The helicopter was almost overhead now, and McKee suddenly realised that the pilot had no way of knowing that he had reached the pick-up point because the beacon wasn't operating, and unless he acted quickly, the Wessex would simply continue on course. He ran into the bedroom and flicked the radio on to transmit.

Calvert unlocked the bedroom door, and standing well to one side, opened it carefully. He pointed the Springfield carbine at David and indicated that he should walk in front of him. McKee might be prepared to link himself to a walking bomb but he was of a more cautious nature. Seven pounds of PE was enough to blow out a wall and bring most of the roof down on top of them; it was also more than sufficient to mangle the pair of them into a bloody, unrecognisable pulp, and he was not going to risk an accidental explosion. He had carefully wrapped the umbilical cord around the boy's neck until he was satisfied that there was not the slightest chance of either of them inadvertently stepping on the trailing lead and actuating the push-pull switch. The boy shuffled out on to the landing; Calvert allowed him to get three paces ahead and then followed him.

As he crept up the last few steps, Tarrant heard McKee say, 'Wessex, unknown call sign, this is Drabble—acknowledge, over.'

A metallic voice answered, 'This is Gulf Echo 221, I read you okay, over.'

'221, you're over the landing site now.'

The pilot wasn't convinced. He said, '221, negative. We have no audio signal from your beacon and no visual sighting of the H panel.'

The anger showed in McKee's voice. '221, use your eyes, you're above me now, turn due south and land in the vicinity of the copse.'

Tarrant reached the landing and froze, appalled at the sight of David. His appearance had changed so much that he scarcely recognised him. The boy's face was ashen beneath the dirt, a strip of grubby sticking plaster covered the cigarette burn on his neck and a filthy bandage covered the fingers on his right hand. His eyes were hollow and dull and he seemed somehow to have shrunk in size.

His son was less than four inches shorter than Calvert and that left precious little for Tarrant to aim at. He brought the Lee Enfield up into his shoulder again and signalled David to get out of the way. He was the very last person David had expected to see and not surprisingly, he was slow to react. The gag turned his cry of recognition into a grunt and he remained frozen like a statue until Calvert, who was still partially un-sighted, urged him forward. He staggered, and as he veered to the left, Calvert noticed Tarrant for the first time. The barrel of the Springfield carbine was pointing down at the floor, and it was still in that position when the first ·303 round smashed into his jaw. The impact turned Calvert through one hundred and eighty degrees and then the second and final round broke his spine.

The mute appeal in his son's eyes laid a claim on him, but as long as the other man remained, Tarrant knew that they were both still in danger. Putting David gently to one side, he went into the room on his right.

McKee was staring at the radio in total disbelief, and he had every reason to. Over and over again, the Wessex pilot repeated, 'Gulf Echo 221, May Day, May Day, May Day, I have power failure, I say again, May Day, May Day, May Day.' McKee spun round to face the intruder and simultaneously his right hand darted for the Browning automatic which he had left on the table. Tarrant grabbed the hot barrel of the Lee Enfield with both hands and felt the metal burn the skin on his palms. He had used every round to come this far and now the empty rifle could only serve but one purpose. He swung it savagely like a club and the butt snapped McKee's wrist as if it were match-wood. The scream rose high and sounded like a flock of gulls.

McKee tried to nurse the injured hand but the second blow dislocated his left elbow and the pain exploded in his skull. And he was defenceless now, and he tried to tell this blond madman that it was all over but the words wouldn't come, and he could only watch helplessly as the rifle swung back again in a vicious arc, and somehow he managed to raise his right arm because he thought the blow would be aimed at his head, but in this he was mistaken and the butt scythed into his right side and the pieces of the shattered rib cage punctured his lung and he staggered backwards until he felt the ledge pressing against his thighs, and even then as he was dying, he saw Tarrant bend down, and hands grabbed him by the ankles, and then he was turning up and over, and the window gave way under his weight, and then he was falling and the hard earth rose up eagerly to meet him and ultimately there was nothing but a deep, black, everlasting void.

And now he could go to his son, and Tarrant's hands were shaking as he untied the gag and began the delicate task of removing the obscene harness, and he was suddenly conscious of the throbbing pain in his left arm where the dog had savaged him, and he felt sick and light-headed when he saw what they had done to David, and the tears were running down his son's face, and he too had to fight hard to hold them back because David was trembling so much that he could scarcely stand upright.

The Wessex, banking sharply as it circled, gave Harper a lop-sided and distorted view of the house below. He caught a fleeting glimpse of Tarrant's car wedged against an open door and close by there was a Mini, and then they were over the front of the house, where he spotted a horse-box parked outside a garage, and then the lane was no longer in sight and instead he had an oblique view of the copse beyond the Dutch barn. The helicopter turned sharply in the other direction and his stomach went with it, and then they were dropping and fluttering as they fell like an autumn leaf.

They landed hard and the crewman shouted something, but Harper didn't hear him clearly because he was busy with his seat belt, and his one concern was to get out through the door as quickly as possible. He followed hard on the heels of the last man in the stick of eight, and although it was totally unnecessary, he kept his head well down until he was clear of the whirling rotor blades. He waved his arms and shouted, and with one accord, the team fanned out into an extended line as they doubled forward. They came on like a row of beaters with Vincent on one flank, Drew on the other and Harper in the centre, and all their carefully rehearsed drills had gone by the board because Tarrant had loused everything up, and Harper's immaculate idea had simply degenerated into a mad, stamped-ing rush.

The blood was pounding in his head and his legs were like lumps of lead and Harper felt sure that he was going to be sick, and then the post-and-rail fence loomed up in front of him and he tried to take it like a steeplechaser but his left foot caught the top rail, and landing awkwardly, he skinned his hands and knees. And then he was up and running again, and out of the corner of his eye he noticed a dead man lying inside the stables, and there was another face down outside the house. His lungs bursting, the sweat pouring off his face, Harper staggered into the hall and saw the bloody shambles around him.

Caution now set in, and he waited there until Drew and Vincent came and joined him, and then he sent them ahead because they were the experts. They moved forward in Indian file but they didn't have far to go. Tarrant, carrying David in his arms, met them in the dining-room.

There was a hostile silence while each man waited for the other to say something. Harper said, 'I'm glad your son is safe.'

Tarrant lowered David into a chair. 'Are you?' he said indifferently.

Harper ignored the implied note of censure. 'I suppose it's too much to hope that you haven't killed them all?' There was no reaction from Tarrant. 'No?' said Harper. 'I rather thought that might be the case. I presume this is what you people in the army call minimum force, is it?'

Tarrant said, 'What did you expect me to do? Shake hands with them?'

'No, but you might have tried to take at least one of them alive. As it is, we have missed out on a lot of valuable information.'

'Is there anything else you want to say?' said Tarrant. 'Or can I go home now?'

'Where?'

'The Zephyr is a write-off, but I've got a self-drive Volkswagen parked down the road. I'll pick it up and take David home.'

'Like that?'

'I'll take David to see a doctor first. There should be one in Melton Basset.'

'You'll never make it on your own. Drew will drive you into the village.'

'Thank you.'

'I wish,' said Harper, in a moment of rare childish irritation, 'I wish I could say the same.'

'Don't let it worry you,' said Tarrant, 'I won't take offence if you don't.' He stooped and picked David up in his arms and carried him out into the yard.

They were a little short on transport but the Mini-Cooper was available, and Drew, who was good at that sort of thing, by-passed the ignition circuit at the switch with a piece of wire. It wouldn't do the car a lot of good but there was no one to complain about that. They stopped by the call-box at the end of the lane and Tarrant got the operator to put through a person to person call, and it seemed an age before Alex answered, and when he told her that David was safe, she started to cry, and she was still half crying, half laughing, when David spoke to her, but it didn't matter that they were almost incoherent because the nightmare was over and Tarrant knew that they had come together again, and this time it would last. And Drew, who was watching them from the car, saw the emotion in their faces and turned away because he suddenly felt embarrassed.

A small army of men had gone through the house and cleared everything away, and Harper had made sure that Julyan's body was removed in the Wessex helicopter long before the ambulance men arrived, because he was determined that news of the intended defection should not leak out. Tarrant and the aircrew were bound by the Official Secrets Act, and he had no fears about Alex either because in his own mind, he was certain that once David had been returned to her, she would not be interested in the whys and wherefores.

To keep the Press at bay, he had authorised an initial release which merely gave the bald facts. Later, one or two of his own people would come forward as witnesses and the police investigation would show that one of the kidnappers had gone berserk under the influence of drugs. It would be a work of fiction, but he believed that it would stand up under scrutiny.

Seated there in the lounge with a glass of Burroughs' whisky in his hand, Harper had reason to be pleased with the end result, and yet a tiny seed of discontent remained.

He looked at Vincent across the room, and without any preamble said, 'What do you make of Tarrant?'

Vincent considered the question carefully. 'I wouldn't like to get on the wrong side of him,' he said.

'Any reservations about him?'

'I'm not sure.'

'Neither am I,' said Harper. 'Every time something happens I see that man in a different light. He's like a chameleon, his colour changes with the background, and there's no one left who could either prove or disprove his innocence. He killed them all.' He shook his head regretfully. 'It's all very untidy.'

'His son looked in a bad way.'

'Yes, he did. If Tarrant was a party to the affair, some of his associates went further than he thought they would.'

'A bit far-fetched, isn't it?' said Vincent.

'Possibly, but I'd still like to be a hundred per cent sure of him.'

'I see.'

'I don't think you do,' Harper said briskly. 'I want you to keep him under tight surveillance for the next twelve months.'

'And if he is bent?'

'The CIA have a curious expression—they speak of terminating with utmost hostility.'

'And how do we put it?' Vincent said quietly.

'Oh, we don't go in for that sort of thing,' Harper said hastily.

There was a long pause, and then, for no reason except perhaps that he had a deep and abiding interest in the game, Harper said, 'I wonder if we shall retain The Ashes?'

CORONET MAKE YOU SOME OFFERS

All these books are available at your bookshop or newsagent, or can be ordered direct from the publisher. Just tick the titles you want and fill in the form below.

CORONET BOOKS, P.O. Box 11, Falmouth, Cornwall.

Please send cheque or postal order. No currency, and allow the following for postage and packing:
1 book—7p per copy, 2–4 books—5p per copy, 5–8 books—4p per copy, 9–15 books—2½p per copy, 16–30 books—2p per copy in U.K., 7p per copy overseas.

Name ....

Address ....

....